Longlisted – Guardian Children's Fiction Prize

'Moving, funny and beautifully written.'
Book Trust

'Natasha Farrant is exceptional at capturing the details of family life and the swirling emotions that surround them.'
Julia Eccleshare, *Lovereading*

'Sweet, funny, heart-warming and just plain wonderful. If you haven't read *After Iris* and *Flora in Love* you're seriously missing out.'
So Many Books, So Little Time

'There's a recognition that things don't always go right in life; yet the tone of the novel remains light, optimistic and good-humoured. *Flora in Love* is a winner! Read it!'
We Love This Book

'*Flora in Love* is everything I wanted it to be; happy, worried, it made me cheer and cry with laug...
Luna...

'Hugely recommended as one of the sweetest and funniest contemporaries of a great year for the genre! I can't ... book three.'
...eah Yeah

About the Author

Natasha Farrant has worked in children's publishing for almost twenty years, running her own literary scouting agency for the past ten. She is the author of the Bluebell Gadsby series and the Carnegie-longlisted and Branford Boase-shortlisted YA historical novel *The Things We Did For Love*, as well as two successful adult novels. Natasha was shortlisted for the Queen of Teen Award 2014, and the second Bluebell Gadbsy book, *Flora in Love*, was longlisted for the Guardian Children's Fiction Prize.

She grew up in London where she still lives with her husband, their two daughters and a large, tortoiseshell cat. She is the eldest of four siblings and has never kept pet rats.

By the same author

The Bluebell Gadsby series
After Iris
All About Pumpkin

The Things We Did For Love

Natasha Farrant

FABER & FABER

First published in 2014
by Faber & Faber Limited
Bloomsbury House,
74–77 Great Russell Street,
London WC1B 3DA
This edition first published in 2015

Typeset by Faber & Faber Ltd

Printed by CPI Group (UK) Ltd, Croydon CR0 4YY

A CIP record for this book
is available from the British Library

ISBN 978-0-571-32696-9

FSC
www.fsc.org
MIX
Paper from
responsible sources
FSC® C101712

2 4 6 8 10 9 7 5 3 1

For Sophie, Steph and Pierre

Love, always

Being a combination of conventional diary entries and transcripts of short films shot by the author on the camera she was given for her thirteenth birthday, beginning at the end of summer.

The Film Diaries of Bluebell Gadsby

Scene One (Transcript)
Sunday Dinner

INTERIOR. EVENING.

The Gadsby family kitchen in the basement of the big house in Chatsworth Square is a mess. Bubbling pans crowd the hob. A collapsed chocolate cake balances on top of a fruit bowl. The sink is piled high with dirty dishes. Water drips, steady and unnoticed, on to the floor. FATHER lays the table, looking grumpy. FLORA sits at one end of the sofa under the window. She wears leopard-print leggings, an emerald-green sweater and the fedora she has refused to take off since she had her hair cropped and dyed peroxide blonde last week on her seventeenth birthday. She is reading a play. At the other end of the sofa, nine-year-old JASMINE is her complete opposite – tiny, with tangled black hair falling down to her waist, a long black tunic over black jeans, and silver high tops. She is reading a poem called *The Raven* by Edgar Allan Poe.

MOTHER, covered in flour and melted chocolate, stands by the cooking range. She is flustered. She tastes the contents of a pan (tonight she is making goulash), burns her tongue and throws the spoon in the sink.

NOTE 1: For the past year, Sunday night dinner has been prepared by Zoran, the Gadsby family's au pair, who started out being able to cook nothing but sausages but by the time he moved out a month ago had become a seriously good cook. He is coming for dinner tonight for the first time since he left to become a full-time music teacher, and Mother is determined to make an impression.

                    FATHER
        I should be writing my book. I
      should not be laying tables. Remind
        me again why we are doing this?

                    FLORA
         (smirks, still reading her play)
        Mum wants to show us she cooks just
                as well as Zoran.

                    MOTHER
        I am simply throwing together a meal
                for an old friend.

                    FATHER
        It doesn't look simple to me, it
                    looks . . .

                    MOTHER
                    What?

                    FATHER
                  Excessive.

        Mother glares at Father. For a moment,
        it looks like she is going to throw

                        3

the goulash at his head, but then a football sails in through the garden door (left open despite the cold night air because it is so hot in the kitchen), followed by TWIG.

The football crashes into the laid table and breaks several glasses.

NOTE 2: Since Twig turned eleven last summer, the family joke is that his legs have grown so fast he doesn't know what to do with them. And sure enough, no sooner does Twig burst into the room after the ball than he trips over his legs and ends up sprawled on the floor, leaving a trail of mud and wet leaves.

TWIG
(somewhat awestruck by the damage
he has done)
I swear I didn't do that on purpose.

The telephone rings. Mother answers, looking increasingly dejected as she murmurs phrases like 'of course I understand' and 'please let us know if there is anything we can do to help'.

MOTHER
(hangs up the phone, looking like
she wants to cry)
That was Zoran. Someone has had a
heart attack. He's not coming.

FATHER
(surveying the ruined table)
After all that?

MOTHER
David, someone has had a *heart
attack*.

She notices CAMERAMAN (Blue) for the
first time.

MOTHER
Blue, what are you doing with that
camera?

CAMERAMAN
I'm starting up my diary again.

MOTHER
Turn it off, *now*.

I have noticed that people only write in diaries when there's something wrong, write properly I mean. Over the past few months I've only used up about half a notebook, and most of those entries are all 'I can't believe how long it's been since I last wrote' or 'Oh dear I feel guilty because the holidays are over and I haven't once opened this notebook,' but today I have got right back into it because Mum and Dad are fighting again. Last year, when Zoran came to live with us as our au pair, we were falling apart because my twin sister Iris had died three years before and we still missed her so much, but things started to get better after he arrived. In fact, they improved so much that when he tried to resign last Christmas, we wouldn't let him go. Even after Mum and Dad decided to leave their old jobs so they could be at home more (Dad is a full-time writer and Mum works for a smaller cosmetics company that doesn't make her travel), he stayed with us right up until the summer, when he finally completed his PhD in Medieval History and told us it was time for him to move on.

'I cannot be a nanny for ever,' he explained when we asked him why. He has been giving music lessons all year, and now he wants to be a full-time music teacher.

At first, after Mum and Dad resigned, they made a real effort, not just with us but with each other. They stopped fighting and started to slope off for romantic weekends in the country instead. Apparently they had a lot of catching up to do, and it just wasn't possible to be romantic with four children in the house. Flora said it was a scandal. She said that at her age she was the one who was supposed to be skulking off to canoodle in secret, and that they were making a complete spectacle of themselves, but they were happy, so we didn't mind. And then, round about when Zoran left, Mum and Dad's canoodling stopped. This morning they had a huge fight, and they have barely spoken to each other all day. Flora says we should Resign Ourselves to the Inevitable. We were all quite ready for the parents to divorce last Christmas, and apparently the intervening months have been no more than a Temporary Reprieve.

I don't know if Zoran leaving and Mum and Dad quarrelling are related. I just know that even though he wasn't always very good at looking after us, things were better at home when he was still around.

The reason Zoran didn't come for dinner is that

the grandfather of one of his students has had a stroke. The difference between a heart attack and a stroke, Dad says, is that a heart attack is what happens when blood stops flowing to the heart, and a stroke is what happens when blood stops flowing to the brain.

'So it's a brain attack,' Twig said, and Dad said yes, he supposed it was.

'But why does that mean Zoran couldn't come for dinner?' Jas frowned.

'Because he was at the boy's house giving a music lesson when it happened. The boy lives with his grandfather and has no other family. Zoran offered to look after him.' Mum stared at the goulash, the green beans, the potato gratin, the red cabbage with apples and raisins, the chocolate cake and the custard, and sighed.

'Those poor people,' she said.

'Is the grandfather going to die?' Jas is fascinated by death. 'Will the boy be an orphan?'

'I'm sure it won't come to that,' Mum said. 'Please stop asking questions.'

'I still don't get why they couldn't come for dinner,' Twig said.

Flora said, 'Oh, what, Zoran should have been like, I know your only relative just nearly died but why don't you come and have dinner with a group of total strangers?'

'We're not strangers,' Twig said.

'I can't imagine only having one relative,' I said. 'That's so sad.'

As usual, nobody listened to me except for Mum, who gave me a little smile. Zoran says every family has a child who is less loud than the others, and sometimes I feel like I'm invisible. Maybe it's because unlike Flora and Jas, I don't have statement hair and clothes. My hair is brown and normal, my clothes never seem to go together and at fourteen I'm still wearing the little round glasses I got when I was twelve, but I don't really care about any of that. I just wish once in a while someone would pay attention when I finally get a word in edgeways.

'But why is Zoran looking after him?' Jas ploughed on. 'I thought he didn't want to be a nanny any more. If he was still living with us, would that mean the boy with the grandfather would come and live here too? Couldn't they come and live here anyway?'

'STOP ASKING QUESTIONS!' said Dad.

'She's only asking because she wants to know,' said Mum.

'You just told her exactly the same thing.'

'That was different.'

'No it wasn't.'

'Yes it was.'

'Sometimes,' Jas said, 'I wish *I* were an orphan.'

'That is a terrible thing to say,' Flora scolded, but then she added that sometimes she did too, and everybody sulked for the rest of the evening.

Monday 4 November (the first day of half-term)

Jake has asked me to go out with him. He left for Australia today, to go to his cousin's wedding. The holidays are only a week long, but because Australia is so far away and it is A Genuine Family Reason as well as a Highly Educational Trip, God (aka Mr Kelly the headmaster) has given Special Dispensation for him to stay away for a month. On Friday Tom, who along with Colin is still Jake's best friend for reasons I sometimes find hard to understand, was all WHAHAY, DUDE, NO SCHOOL FOR A MONTH AND THINK OF ALL THOSE HOT SURF CHICKS but Jake went all serious and then this morning he said could I meet him at the Home Sweet Home cafe before he went to the airport and he asked me.

Clearly, I am not invisible to Jake.

'The thought of a whole month without you', he said, 'made me realise how much I like you.' He asked if I would wait for him and I nearly choked over my cappuccino because even though I've known Jake since primary school, I have never thought about him in that way and it was the last thing I expected him to say. He taught me to skateboard last year when I was still so unhappy about Iris, and he's been one of my best friends ever since, but being best friends with someone is not the same as going out with them. I was trying to find a way of telling him that but then he said, 'Blue, are you OK?' and he looked so worried and nervous that instead I said yes, going out with him would be very nice.

As soon as I got home I climbed on to the flat roof outside my bedroom window to call Dodi (it's the only place in our house where you can be really private). Dodi is about as different from me as a best friend can get. She's blonde and girly, she loves fashion, and even though she's never actually had a boyfriend, she's very interested in boys.

'Tell me exactly what happened,' Dodi said.

'He said would I wait for him, and then he kissed

me on the cheek and held my hand for a bit and made me promise to email him every day.'

Dodi sighed and said that made us practically married.

'It wasn't very passionate,' I said.

Dodi says that's because we are such good friends. She says it's hard to be passionate when you know someone so well, but after a month apart, the flames of our passion will be *incandescent*.

Seriously. Incandescent. Dodi is the sort of person who has an opinion on everything. I can't imagine how it would feel to be like her, always so sure that you are right.

'So you think I should go out with him?' I asked.

'You've already said yes, haven't you?' She sounded really excited. I tried to explain about friends not being the same as boyfriends and everything, but as well as always having opinions, Dodi also often doesn't listen to me.

'You two are going to make the cutest couple,' she said, but then our conversation was interrupted by my family starting to scream at each other in the garden.

'What's going on *now*?' Dodi's parents are very quiet and she doesn't have any brothers or sisters. She is endlessly fascinated by us.

I crept to the edge of the roof. Beneath me, Dad stood by Twig and Jas's pet rats' cage, surrounded by the rest of my family, who were all yelling.

'I'll call you back,' I told Dodi.

What happened was, Dad let the rats escape this morning. Normally Jas feeds them, but she was staying with her friend Lola last night, so Dad said he would do it but then he forgot to close the cage and they ran away. Jas found the cage wide open when she came home.

Dad tried to defend himself, saying the rats were probably happier living free as God intended. Jas cried, 'But they are not used to the wild.' Dad said Chatsworth Square was not exactly the wild and Jas started to sob that her heart was broken for ever, which is when Mum jumped in saying, 'Really, David, murdering the children's pets is the last straw.'

'1 did not *murder* them!' cried Dad. 'It was an accident! And they are rats! They can live anywhere!'

All seven of the rats have escaped. Twig, who had promised to sell Betsy's babies to his friends, informed Dad he had ruined his career. Jas cried even harder because she hadn't even realised Betsy was pregnant, but nobody was listening to her because Dad was yelling, 'Freedom! Freedom!' like some deranged rat revolutionary. Mum said he couldn't use political idealism as an excuse, especially applied to rats, and then he started waving his arms around crying how no one understands how difficult it is for him to be locked in his study all day trying to write a novel and knowing that the responsibility for his ENTIRE FAMILY'S WELL-BEING rests on his shoulders, and we all tiptoed away because it was clear our father had finally lost his mind.

I emailed Jake before writing this, to tell him all about it. Now that I have agreed to go out with him, I feel that I should tell him everything, even though it's not always easy to find the words. Nobody wants people to think their father is a lunatic. Then I called Zoran to see if he could help, but he says there is nothing he can do. Rats, once they are gone, are gone for ever, in Zoran's opinion.

His student's grandfather from last night, who is called Mr Rudowski, hasn't woken up from his stroke yet. His student, who is called Zach, is still staying with him because even though Zoran has tried to call the boy's mother, she hasn't replied.

'Zach says she lives abroad,' he said.

'How come he lives with his grandfather?' I asked.

Zoran said it was complicated.

'Why hasn't she replied?'

'I don't know, Blue. Believe me, I wish she would.'

I wish Zoran would come home and live with us, but unlike Jas, I have no desire to be an orphan. I'd rather have two parents yelling at each other than no parents at all.

Thursday 7 November

Jas came to find me in my room this afternoon, and I knew something was up because she didn't comment on my wall, which I have spent the whole day painting from floor to ceiling with metallic silver radiator paint. This is the sort of thing you do when your grandmother, who you would normally spend half-term with, decides to defy the passing of the years by going on a three-month riding holiday in Arizona. I was just working on the final coat when she slunk in (Jas, not Grandma) and said, 'You have to help me.'

'If I stop now,' I told her, 'I will forget where I got to, and the paint will be uneven. Go and ask Flora.'

'Flora is at a play audition. I'm not supposed to know.'

None of us are supposed to know about Flora's play auditions, because Flora is not supposed to be going to them. Flora is doing her A levels in June, and all theatrical engagements are Strictly Banned.

'What about Twig?'

Jas's expression darkened.

'He's gone to have his hair cut,' she sniffed.

As well as suddenly becoming tall, Twig is obsessed with how he looks. It makes Jas cross because she says he never has time to play any more. We always used to call the two of them together the Babes, but that's all changed now, mainly because they no longer ever seem to *be* together.

'It could be worse,' I tried to cheer her up. 'He could be one of those boys who never wash at all.'

'It's disgusting. It's all because of stupid Maisie Carter at school. He fancies her. You *have* to help me.'

'I *have* to finish painting my room.'

'Then I'll stay until you change your mind,' she said, and she sat down on the floor.

'I'm ignoring you,' I told her.

'Fine,' she replied.

I stopped feeling her glare at me after a while and

had almost forgotten she was there when suddenly she said, 'I found two kittens in the graveyard,' and I dropped my paintbrush.

There is a spray of silver paint all over my bedroom floor, but under the circumstances it hardly seems to matter. The graveyard is several streets away, and though I don't think anyone has ever told us not to go there, I'm also fairly certain it's not a place Jas should be going to on her own.

'What were you doing in the graveyard?' I asked.

'I go there quite often,' she answered. 'It's quiet, and there's a lovely gravestone of an old lady called Violet Buttercream where I like to sit.'

'Violet Buttercream?'

Jas told me I was missing the point.

'I've hidden them in the shed,' she said. 'And you have to come *now*.'

So much for eternal heartbreak. I think she's already forgotten all about the rats.

Saturday 9 November

There wasn't time to finish writing about the kittens last night. Orphaned kittens need constant attention, which is particularly difficult if you have to keep them a secret.

'Why?' I asked. 'Why do they have to be secret?'

'Because they're *mine*,' she growled. 'Dad would let them run away, and Twig would probably try to sell them.'

'But are you quite sure they don't have a mother?'

'I've been watching them for two days. She never usually leaves them for more than a few minutes, but today she didn't come back for hours. I think something must have happened to her.'

So now the kittens have a nest of their own in the shed. We plugged an electric radiator in so they wouldn't get cold and we filled a cardboard crate with old fleeces and blankets, and then we went to the pet shop where Jas bought a litter tray, cat litter and kitten food with money out of her savings. The kittens are the scrawniest creatures I ever saw, but they are also completely adorable. There are two of them, a boy and a girl, and they are completely black with green eyes and enormous black whiskers, which look much too big for their bodies. Jas made me take a photograph of them on my phone to show the girl in the pet shop, who says they are about twelve weeks old. She also says Jas should take them to the vet, but Jas says that's too expensive.

I don't know how long she thinks she can keep them secret. Zoran came round to see us this afternoon. He came on his new electric scooter that Flora thinks is ridiculous, but even though it normally makes him really happy, he looked so depressed when he walked in that the first thing Jas did was drag him out to the shed to show him.

'I've named the boy Ron,' she said. 'And the girl is called Hermione.'

'They're adorable,' said Zoran, but he looked really glum. We went back into the kitchen where Twig, who for reasons nobody knows is teaching himself to bake, was pulling a tray of perfect raisin and hazelnut cookies out of the oven, but even that didn't cheer Zoran up. As we ate them, Flora told us all about her audition. She is down to the last three for a small but *very important* role in a West End production, but we're still not allowed to tell the parents about it. She went through the plot down to the minutest detail, and then she said, 'All right Zoran, what's wrong, you haven't been listening to a word I said.'

'*Nobody* has listened to a word you said,' Twig pointed out.

'Is that boy still staying with you?' Flora asked.

Zoran sighed and said he needed our advice. Mr

Rudowski woke up from his stroke this morning, but he can't come home yet. Instead, they are moving him out of London to a hospital in the country where they will teach him to walk and eat and sit up again, because one half of his body has forgotten how to do all these things. He has asked Zoran if Zach could carry on living with him 'until other arrangements can be made'.

'What other arrangements?' Flora asked.

'Until his mother gets in touch, I suppose.' He explained again what he'd already told me, that he'd tried calling her but that she still hadn't replied. He also said that she and Zach had lived with her parents ever since Zach's father left them when he was little, but that was two years ago. After Zach's grandmother died, there had been a quarrel and ever since his mother and grandfather have been estranged.

'She left Zach with his grandfather and they haven't seen her since,' Zoran said.

'What does estranged mean?' Jas wanted to know.

'They don't talk to each other.'

'*Ever?*' Jas looked appalled.

'What about Zach?' Twig asked. 'Does he talk to her?'

'I know they email occasionally, but he hasn't heard from her either.'

'What did you say to Mr Rudowski?' Flora demanded. 'Did you say you would do it?'

'Well how could I say no?' Zoran asked. 'Poor kid, it's either me or a foster family he doesn't know. And I like Mr Rudowski. He's still in mourning for his wife, and he doesn't talk much, but he's a kind old man and he's a friend of Auntie Alina's. She's the one who put us in touch.'

Alina is Zoran's great-aunt, who brought him up when he came to live in England after escaping the war in Bosnia. Zoran adores her.

'So you *are* going to be his nanny.' Jas's lower lip started to wobble.

'Not his nanny, exactly,' Zoran said 'A seventeen-year-old boy doesn't need a *nanny*. More a guardian, I suppose. And just for a short time. It's not like it was with you. You do understand, don't you, Jas? He needs me.'

'Like you looking after the kittens,' I whispered in her ear.

Jas nodded reluctantly.

'You said you needed our advice,' Flora said.

Zoran sighed, and said that he had always liked Zach but the problem was there was a big difference between teaching a person for an hour a week and them actually living with you, and how could he get Zach to talk to him? 'At the moment,' Zoran said, 'he barely acknowledges me at all. I understand that he's worried and angry, of course, but this morning he wouldn't even have breakfast! He just said he wasn't hungry.'

'I never have breakfast,' Flora said.

'I made *pancakes*!' Zoran looked so indignant we all had to try really hard not to laugh at him. 'I'm not used to not getting on with people,' he said. 'I thought I was good with teenagers.'

'You can't lump all teenagers together, like we're all exactly the same,' Flora lectured. 'We're people too, you know. You can't get on with every single one of us, just because you think you're *good with us*.'

'And sometimes people don't want to be helped,' I added. 'You can't make them talk if they don't want to.'

'Is he playing in your concert?' Twig asked.

Zoran has got a load of his students working towards a sort of family concert, except us because Flora says it will be terrible and we all secretly agree. If our own musical standard after nearly a year of lessons is anything to go by, I don't hold out much hope for his other students.

Zoran said he had asked him, but Zach had said no.

'Flatter him,' Flora advised. 'Boys love that. Tell him the concert will be rubbish without him.'

'We'll all come to support you,' I said. 'We'll all cheer him like crazy and he'll feel amazing and it'll be like an unbreakable bond between you.'

'Either that or everyone'll hate him and he'll never speak to you again,' Flora said.

'He's not speaking to him anyway,' Twig reminded us, and Flora said that was true, so there was nothing to lose.

Zoran looked unconvinced, but said that he would give it another try.

Sunday 10 November

Today I got an email from Jake in which he told me that the weather in Australia is awesome and that surfing is a bit like skateboarding but a lot more wet.

Yesterday was his cousin's wedding. They had their reception on the beach and all the wedding guests did a giant conga in the sea, and apparently that was awesome too. He also said my emails are hilarious and he reads them out loud to all his

Australian relatives, who nearly died laughing over Dad releasing the rats and say my family is nuts, which I am not very happy about, because even though it's a little bit true, it's not for him to say so.

'Plus it's not very romantic,' Dodi agreed when I told her. She told me I should write back straight away and tell Jake that while I'm glad his relations find me so entertaining, our correspondence is *supposed* to be private.

'That makes it sound like I'm cross with him,' I said.

'Well you *are* cross with him,' Dodi replied. I said yes, but I didn't want to hurt his feelings, and Dodi said that was a little bit pathetic.

This whole boyfriend business is so complicated, and Jake isn't even in the same *country*.

Tuesday 12 November

Ron and Hermione are living up to their magical names.

Today I had to go and collect Jas from Zoran's flat when I got home from school, because she ran away there after a row with Dad. Zoran called to let us know she was there.

'I don't know what is wrong with that child,' Dad grumbled when I came home from school. 'You all know not to interrupt me when I'm writing, but she barged in when I was right in the middle of an extremely difficult chapter and when I asked her to leave she just stormed off. I didn't realise she'd actually left the house.'

Zoran's flat is only a ten-minute walk from us, but where Chatsworth Square is all leafy and peaceful with the big communal garden in the middle, the road he lives on has shops and buses and there are always people about. He lives in a big old converted house, right on the top floor, and he has this window seat which feels like a sort of bird's nest because when you look outside you're completely surrounded by trees. I was a bit apprehensive as I walked up the stairs thinking this would be the moment when I finally got to meet Zach, which was sort of exciting but also a bit worrying because I couldn't think what to say to him without giving away that Zoran had been talking about him behind his back. But then Zoran opened the door and I went in and the boy wasn't there and the flat looked just like it always does, with shelves crammed with books and the pictures Alina gave him when she sold her house to go into her nursing home. The radio was playing piano music, and there was the smell of Earl Grey tea and fresh paint and blue flowers in a pot, and Jas was curled up wearing one of Zoran's sweaters and wrapped in a duvet, pretending to do homework but really playing with the kittens who were tumbling in and out of Zoran's guitar case next to her on the sofa.

'I don't know what you're doing here,' she said. 'I'm perfectly capable of walking home on my own.'

'How on earth did you get the kittens here?' I asked.

'In my pockets,' she said, like it was obvious.

'Your sister got caught in the rain,' Zoran told me. 'She was soaked to the skin when she got here.'

Zoran hates it when Jas goes wandering off. He started on this whole lecture about how in fact Jas is still very small and has to learn to do what she is told, and how the rest of us really ought to look after her properly. He didn't even notice when Hermione rolled off the bed, padded across the carpet and started to climb up his trouser leg.

'It was pure luck two of my students cancelled this afternoon and I happened to be in. Pure luck!' Zoran scolded.

'Where is the boy?' I asked to distract him.

'He has football practice on Tuesdays.'

I curled up next to Jas and tickled Ron, who started to purr, sounding like he might just burst out of pure excitement. It's quite unbelievable that something so small can make so much noise. Then I looked round the flat again and noticed that unlike Ron, the boy Zach hadn't made his presence felt at all.

'Where are all his things?' I asked. 'Can I see his room?'

'It's private,' Zoran said, and then he screamed as Hermione sank her fangs into his hand and started pedalling against his wrist with her back claws.

Kitten claws are surprisingly sharp.

I know Zoran said I shouldn't, but his spare bedroom is one of my favourite rooms in the world, and I couldn't resist seeing what it looked like with someone actually living in it. It's tiny, not much bigger than a cupboard. When Zoran first moved in he thought about just using it as a study or something, but then he decided that he really wanted somewhere people could come and stay, like his sister who lives in Sarajevo. So he bought a bed which fits perfectly across the width of the room under the window, and he put up hooks and shelves and even a fold-down table, painted the walls a soft pale blue like the sky and hung those green and red glass balls you find at the seaside. It's like a ship's cabin, with a space for everything, but when I opened the door I was disappointed, because it looked exactly the same, but with clothes and school books dumped all over the floor and nothing hanging up.

'It's like he can't be bothered.'

'I told you, he's not exactly overjoyed about our arrangement,' Zoran said, and then he added, 'I need you to take Jas and these animals home. My hand is actually bleeding.'

'Is he going to play in your concert?'

'No, he is not. Apparently, he doesn't *do* concerts.'

Zoran picked up Hermione so her tummy was on his hand with her little legs and her head sticking out the side, so she couldn't hurt him again, and held her out to me.

'Ron just weed on your duvet,' said Jas.

Zoran closed his eyes and made this little whining noise. Jas shoved Ron in one coat pocket and Hermione in the other, and we tiptoed out of the flat.

Poor Zoran. He looked so despondent when we left him, with his hands covered in scratches and his duvet covered in kitten wee, but the reason I wrote that Ron and Hermione are living up to their magical names is that when Zach got back he found

Zoran cursing and swearing as he tried to stuff his duvet into the washing machine, and he thought the whole story of the kittens so hilarious he agreed to play in Zoran's concert.

'I think he felt sorry for me,' Zoran said when he called to tell us the news.

'Nobody likes cat pee,' I agreed. 'Did you flatter him, like Flora said?'

Zoran said that was none of my business, but I bet he did. I can just imagine them, Zach laughing his head off, Zoran choosing that exact moment to tell him how stupendously gifted he is. The thing with Zoran is he's so nice, when he wants something you never even realise what you've agreed to till it's too late.

'I suppose I should be grateful to the little beasts,' Zoran said. 'It's the first time I've heard Zach laugh about anything since he got here.'

Jas is acting like she did the whole thing on purpose.

Wednesday 13 November

It's weird being at school without Jake. Today in English Miss Foundry was talking about the Brontë sisters. 'The Yorkshire moors!' she cried. 'The tragedy of tuberculosis! The horrors of contemporary education!' except she has a weak r so it came out as *twagedy* and *howwors of contempowawy education*.

Tom asked, 'Miss, how do you spell *Bwonte*?'

Miss Foundry, who is oblivious to teasing, said with two dots over the e.

'Exactly as I have *witten* it on the whiteboard,' she said, and Tom and Colin both collapsed. I know it's mean, but it gets them every time, and there's something about the way those boys laugh. It spreads, and soon the whole class was shaking. That's when I thought of Jake. Normally there would be three of them messing about in class, but the place right in the middle of the front row, where teachers always make him sit to stop him sleeping or laughing, was empty. Suddenly I could picture exactly what would happen if he had been here, how he would have turned round and grinned at everyone behind him, like making fun of Miss Foundry's pronunciation was still the best joke in the world.

I do kind of miss him, in spite of his unromantic emails.

Zoran came round this afternoon to ask me if I would film the concert. He said it would mean a lot to him.

'I would love to,' I said, because films and their transcripts are an important part of my diaries. Ever since I got my video camera, my plan has been to record my life in words and images, but I don't often get the opportunity to film anyone other than my family.

Flora asked if he had heard from Zach's mother yet, and Zoran said that she had been in touch with her father but there was still no news of when she was coming home.

'You should tell her about the concert,' I told him. 'She'd probably come for that.'

Flora said, 'Do you really think she'd come for Zoran's concert when she's not even been to see her father?'

'She might,' I said.

Zoran said he and Zach had both written to her about the concert.

'Does *he* think she'll come?' I asked.

'That's not really for me to say,' he replied.

Flora said Zach's mother sounded like a total witch.

Mum made pizza this evening for the first time in ages, which meant the kitchen was even more of a mess than usual. She was humming to herself as she cooked, with her hair full of flour. I went straight up to her when she called us down for supper and gave her the biggest hug.

'What's that for?' she asked.

'Just for being you,' I said. Behind me, Twig made a puking noise, but Mum looked really happy. Then Dad came in and she went back to being cross again.

Sunday 17 November

Twig had a football match this afternoon. Mum and Dad had one of their 'you go, no you go, why me, you go' arguments about it, until Flora got involved and informed them that they were *both* going, because today was his first time playing for a real team against another school.

'This is a very important day for him,' she said. 'So whatever is going on between the two of you, you have to get over it.'

There was this moment of shocked silence, and

then Mum said, 'I'll get my bag,' and Dad mumbled, 'I'll get the car keys,' and they both shuffled out behind Twig, who looked a bit startled. Twig isn't actually very good at football and I think he would have liked it better if neither of the parents had been there, but Flora says that doesn't matter.

'It's a question of principle,' she says.

Jas, Flora and I all went to the concert. Me to film, Flora and Jas to cheer for Zach like we had promised, and all three of us because even though none of us will admit it, we were all dying to see what Zachary Smith looked like. The concert took place at Alina's retirement home in Richmond, where Zoran goes once a week to play the piano, and where he now also has a lot of pupils. We all piled into the drawing room, and I began to film.

The Film Diaries of Bluebell Gadsby

Scene Two (Transcript)
The Concert

INTERIOR. AFTERNOON.

The drawing room at Richmond Hill
Retirement Home. Resident students
(all old) sit in armchairs arranged in
a semi-circle around chairs taken from
the dining room, where non-resident
students (mostly children) squirm in
the front rows with their parents
behind them. JAS and FLORA sit at the
back, next to CAMERAMAN (Blue) who is
standing. ZORAN stands to one side at
the front, introducing the musicians
as they come up to play.

*NOTE: To keep things moving along
and in order to get to the really
interesting part of the afternoon,
this transcript is skipping detailed*

descriptions of all the acts, which
included renditions of 'Summertime',
'Frère Jacques', Chopin's Nocturnes,
assorted pieces from the Music
Examination Board's books for Grades
One to Five and a number of current
rock songs. And then, right at the end
. . .

ZORAN
Zachary Smith on guitar, singing
'Broken Birds', a song of his own
creation.

ZACHARY SMITH stands up. Flora, Jas
and even Cameraman crane forward. He
is not at all how they imagined him.
Medium height, slight and pale, with
dark eyes and hair falling over his
face. He wears black jeans, black high
tops and a green-and-black checked
shirt open over an old rock band
T-shirt, and his wrists are covered
in bands and bracelets. He takes his
place at the front and scans the
audience, but it's clear he doesn't
find what he's looking for. His face

drops and he bends over his guitar, taking his time to tune it. His hands are shaking. The moment seems to go on and on. Somebody in the audience giggles. Zoran plays a few notes on the piano and Zach rallies. He strikes a few slow chords and begins to sing.

'Broken bird in my hollowed hand,
Beating heart like you want to shout,
Beating hard to fight your way out,
Broken bird trying to fly,
Where are you going? What do you
want?
Be careful the wind don't blow you
about.

And the waves draw lines upon the
sand, the sand,
The waves draw lines upon the sand,
And when they've drawn them they take
them away,
I hope they take me too some day,
I hope they take me too.

Broken bird, when I let you go
You mustn't look back, you mustn't, no.
Head for the sun and fly right to it,
Look for the light and go straight
through it.
Don't look down or you'll fall and
break,
'Cos the wind ain't gonna carry you
for ever.

And the waves draw lines upon the
sand, the sand, etc.'

The lyrics (in Cameraman's humble opinion) are a bit sentimental, but the melody is simple and haunting and the voice – throaty, rasping but somehow also, when it hits the high notes, pure – holds the audience captive. Zachary Smith finishes. He is still for a moment, holding the silence at the end of the piece. When he looks up, it's like he's come back from a long way away and is a little bit lost.

Camera takes in great-aunt Alina and her
husband Peter, clutching hands, rapt.
Several adult members of the audience are
crying. A lot of the younger kids stare
with their mouths dropped open in amazement
because they never thought one of their
own could ever sing like that. Two older
boys, whose performance of 'Wonderwall' was
unintentionally hilarious, look annoyed.
Camera finally pans to Flora. Flora's mouth
is also open, but she does not look annoyed
or even amazed. Flora's eyes shine. She
leans forward in her chair and she does
not move, even when Zachary Smith stops
singing, but keeps on looking at him like
she cannot believe what she is seeing. He
turns his head towards her. He catches her
eye. Suddenly he doesn't look lost any
more.

He looks - amazed.

Suddenly there is nobody in the room
but him and Flora.

Jas made me replay the whole concert on the Tube on the way home, though we skipped over most of the acts, lingering only on the kid singing 'Summertime' and the old lady playing jazz tunes, until we got to Zach, and then she made me play his bit over and over again. Flora said nothing, just stared out of the Tube window. It was dark outside and there was nothing to see, but I don't think she'd have noticed if a herd of elephants had cantered past playing 'Wonderwall' on the trumpet.

'He's not at all like I expected,' Jas said. Then a little bit later she said, 'I'm glad Zoran's looking after him.'

Flora still said nothing.

Flora, who normally can't shut up for an *instant*. Completely silent.

It was very unnerving.

Monday 18 November

Dad found the kittens this morning, or, more precisely, they found him. Somehow they got out of the shed in the night, and they were stalking up and down outside the kitchen doors when he saw them, mewing for their breakfast.

'AGGGHHHH!' Dad screamed, like they were full-grown tigers instead of seven-week-old kittens.

'MEEEOWWWWW!' the kittens yowled back.

'Oh my God they're adorable!' cried Flora, clapping her hands.

'They're mine,' Jas announced. 'I found them starving in the graveyard and I'm keeping them for ever.'

'We didn't lose the rats to make room for disease-ridden strays,' Dad declared. 'They will have to go.'

'We didn't *lose* the rats, full stop,' Flora reminded him.

'I could sell them,' offered Twig.

'You could not,' snarled Jas.

'This is a very bad time to have new pets,' said Dad. 'Your mother . . .'

'What about me?' Mum wandered down into the kitchen and I have to say that her behaviour at the moment is almost as troubling as Dad's. Normally on a Monday morning she would be tearing around in a suit, ready for work and nagging at us about being late for school, but today she was still in her dressing gown at eight o'clock, eating peanut butter with her fingers straight from the jar.

Jas said, 'It is either the kittens or me.' Dad replied that there were far too many children in the house anyway. Mum walked out, slamming the door.

'That', Flora said to Dad, 'is probably the nastiest thing you have ever said to any of us.'

'I didn't mean it!' cried Dad. He stared from Jas to the door Mum had just stormed out of, then back at Jas again, like he couldn't decide what he should do next. Upstairs we heard another door slam. Dad yelled, 'Just get rid of them!' then sprang into action and tore out after Mum.

'I did mean it!' Jas yelled after him. 'I'll run away again and this time I won't come back!'

'No,' Zoran said when Jas and I trudged round with the kittens this afternoon.

'Just until Daddy calms down,' Jas begged.

'They peed on my duvet!' Zoran cried.

'If you don't take them,' Jas said, 'they will probably die.'

'When are you going to email me your recording?' Zoran asked. 'Loads of people are asking to see it.'

Jas started to scuff the carpet with her foot.

'I would love to email you my recording,' I said, 'but the problem is I can't find my camera.'

Zoran said, 'What do you mean, you can't find it?' and I said, 'I don't know, I've looked everywhere, it's really upsetting,' and then Jas burst into tears and sobbed, 'Oh, who cares about your stupid camera, what about the kittens?' Zoran hugged her but was very firm and said that he would have a word with Mum about them. He went into his bedroom to call her, but we listened at the door. It was hard to hear everything, but basically he told her how good it would be for Jas to look after two needy little animals, especially when things were a bit traumatic.

'What does traumatic mean?' Jas whispered.

'I think he means you're upset because of the rats,' I whispered.

Dad is sulking but Jas is over the moon, because after talking to Zoran Mum said of course the kittens can stay. I think possibly she only said it to annoy Dad, but this makes no difference at all to Jas.

And I've found my camera. It was under Flora's pillow.

'My sister is in love again,' I wrote to Jake this evening. 'She stole my camera after I filmed this boy in a concert he was in and she ran the battery flat watching my recording. I found it under her pillow. Then she went bright red at dinner when Mum asked how the concert went. I'm attaching the clip here so you can see it. Please don't show it to your family.'

I stopped to think while the clip was uploading, and then I wrote, 'On second thoughts, don't take this the wrong way, but I'm not going to send this email, I do hope you understand,' and then instead of pressing send I pressed delete, making today the first day since he went away that I haven't emailed Jake. Sometimes I have really racked my brain to think of something to write and sometimes I have written much too much, but the point is I have written every single day, just like he asked, but he hardly ever writes back and when he does it's always the same thing, about the awesome beach and how funny I am and how amazing it is that it's summer in Australia but winter over here. I told Dodi about it today during break and she said I should write back and say it's not amazing at all, it's just that Australia is in the Southern Hemisphere and we are in the Northern Hemisphere.

It was actually Dodi who said I shouldn't write back. She says that writing back when Jake's answers are so lame makes me look like a pushover. 'Like he's being rude, but you're saying it doesn't matter' were her exact words. I've never thought of it like that before, because I never expected Jake to be much good at writing, but today I did start to think that maybe she was a little bit right.

The Film Diaries of Bluebell Gadsby

Scene Three (Transcript)
The Trouble with Cats

EXTERIOR. MORNING.

On the lawn of the Gadsby family
garden, TWIG in full football kit is
preparing to give a demonstration of
his keepy-uppy skills.

                    DODI
        (in pyjamas, having slept over the
                night before)
        Remind me again why you are doing
                    this.

                CAMERAMAN (BLUE)
        Because I haven't done a sports
                video before.

TWIG

And to prove I can do more than
Justin Murphy.

DODI

Who is Justin Murphy?

JAS

(also in pyjamas, curled up in a
deckchair draped in kittens)
He has the highest record of keepy
uppies in Twig's class; and he is
also in love with Maisie Carter.

DODI

Is Twig in love with Maisie Carter?

JAS

He tried baking cookies for her but
apparently she is allergic to
hazelnuts.

TWIG

(glaring at Jas)
Can we get on with it?

                           JAS
                    (smiles sweetly)
           Be my guest. I'm just here to count
             and make sure you don't cheat.

Twig places the ball at his feet, then
flicks it up to his knees. Bounces
it off his right knee. Bounces it
off his left knee. He has obviously
been practising. A lot. Right, left,
right, left. Right ankle. Left knee.
Chest. Head. Left knee. Right knee.
Jas counts each keepy uppy. Dodi
yawns, loudly. Jas giggles and
announces she's lost count and they
have to start again. Twig tells her the
whole thing is filmed anyway and they
don't need her. Jas tells him one day
he'll be sorry he ever said that. Twig
almost drops the ball but recovers
manfully with a skilful sideways flick
of the left ankle. He looks triumphant
but drops the ball when from the
open bathroom window two storeys above
comes the sound of someone shouting
AAAAAAAGGGGGGGGGGGGGGGGGHHHHHHHHHHHHHHH!

FATHER

(his disembodied voice floating down
from the window)

Jas! JAS!! Where is that child?

Jas vaults out of her deckchair and
tries to hide behind it, kittens and
all.

TWIG

She's out here!

DODI

You're a rat, Twig Gadsby. I hope
you know that.

CAMERAMAN

It's best not to mention rats in
this family.

Sound of footsteps on the stairs,
culminating in Father erupting into
the garden, clad in nothing but a
miniature towel which he holds around
his waist with one hand. He marches
towards Jas with his other hand
extended before him, thumb and

forefinger curiously pinched together,
and opens them when he reaches her.

                    FATHER
                    Well?

                    JAS
        (understandably looking like Father
                is deranged)
        It's a black dot. Oh! It's a black
                dot that moves!

                    FATHER
        It's a flea! It's a flea!! Your cats
            have given me fleas!!!

Dodi gasps, and almost immediately
begins to scratch her head. Father
yells, 'You see? We've all got them!'
He slaps at something on his arm,
accidentally letting go of his towel.
Dodi gasps again.

                    FATHER
        TURN THAT ****** CAMERA OFF, BLUE!!

Cameraman complies, but before she

does, another sound floats down from above. Picture pans up to the bathroom window, where MOTHER and FLORA stand, clutching each other, tears of laughter pouring down their faces at the sight of Father's naked bottom.

Dad tried to order us all to clean the house after finding the fleas, but I escaped by telling him I had promised to go round to Zoran's to talk about making edits to my recording (which was true). Dodi came with me. She said she had nothing better to do, but I know that ever since she saw him on film she has been dying to meet Zach.

'He works on Saturday mornings,' I told her. 'He has a job at the old record shop on the Avenue.'

Dodi, who is an eternal optimist, said she was coming anyway.

Zoran said he was very pleased with my recording, and could I just cut down all the bits in between pieces, the applause and the tuning up and so forth, to make it a little bit shorter.

'Oh, and take out that bit with Flora and Zach,' he added. 'There's far too much footage of them looking at each other.'

Dodi protested that was the best bit. Zoran said it was inappropriate.

'You *can't* get rid of that footage,' Dodi said as we ran downstairs. 'It would be criminal. It would be a waste. It would be a *criminal waste*.'

And then we both stopped talking, because *he* was coming up the stairs towards us.

Zachary Smith.

Who Flora's in love with.

He stopped in front of us. 'Oh,' he said. Then, 'You're the one with the camera.'

'She is indeed,' Dodi drawled when I couldn't think of an answer.

'With the kittens,' said Zach.

'They're my little sister's.'

'Cool,' he stammered. And then he looked embarrassed and mumbled about having forgotten something and being late for work, and ran off up the stairs.

'Very, very odd,' commented Dodi.

'Most peculiar,' I agreed.

'Do you think he was trying to charm you? Like he's hoping you'll tell Flora how dreamy he is, and what witty conversational skills he has?'

We both sniggered at that. I know it's not nice.

Dodi said she was disappointed in Zach in real life. She said that when he wasn't singing or casting smouldering looks at Flora, he looked like a bit of a loser. I said that he reminded me of the poet Keats, who we studied in English before the Bwontës, and who died tragically young in Italy of tuberculosis.

Dodi, who never lets anything she learns at school follow her into real life, said she would never have thought about that, but that she supposed he did remind her of all sorts of doomed rock stars, and perhaps that is what Flora saw in him.

Dad has spent the whole day cleaning. The house is draped with drying bed linen from basement to attic, and I have never seen it sparkle so much. At dinner, he announced again that we had to get rid of the kittens, but Mum said no.

Dad said the kittens kept disturbing him when he was trying to work.

'In this family,' Mum said, 'we look after the weak and the vulnerable. In fact,' Mum added, 'we don't just look after them, we *welcome* them.' She sounded really fierce, and also like she wasn't really talking about kittens at all. I think Dad realised that too, because he didn't answer but looked down when she glared at him.

The kittens have been rolled in flea powder like two little doughnuts in icing sugar, and they are not allowed out of the kitchen.

The Very Much Enhanced Film Diaries of Bluebell Gadsby

Scene Four (Transcript)
Love at First Sight

INTERIOR. AFTERNOON.

ZACHARY SMITH sits on a chair, playing his guitar. His surroundings (the Richmond Hill Retirement Home) have vanished in a misty haze. All background noise has been edited out. The only sound is that of his singing and strumming. Picture cuts to FLORA, gazing at him. A ribbon of pink cartoon hearts floats from her mouth to form a bubble above her head, inside which, in yellow letters, is the single word SIGH. Zach, in his misty haze, is enveloped in a cloud of baby-blue songbirds. Think Disney's Cinderella and all the little animals. His speech bubble says, YOU'RE BEAUTIFUL. When the song reaches the chorus – *And the waves draw lines upon the sand, the sand* – the picture switches briefly to a tropical sunset and a couple running together in the water, then returns to a split screen with Zach on one side, looking poetically tragic, and Flora on the other, smiling with her eyes closed in apparent ecstasy. The picture melts away as the music fades and the following words take over the screen:

ZACH AND FLORA
LOVE
AT
FIRST
SIGHT

It was all Dodi's idea. I'm not saying I didn't want to go along with it, or that I'm not glad I did. We spent the whole day turning Zach and Flora gazing at each other at the concert into a full-length music video. I learned a ton of things. The end result was fabulous.

It just wasn't my idea to put it on YouTube.

Flora has a history with YouTube. Last year, her then horrible boyfriend's even more horrible friends uploaded a film of Flora playing one of Snow White's Seven Dwarves in a Christmas show, when her leather shorts split as she was doing a forward bend. It was a very poor-quality video, but it was unmistakably Flora, and she was unmistakably not wearing anything under the shorts.

'But this is not humiliating at all,' Dodi reasoned. 'This is tasteful and romantic.' And then she said that our clip could be seen by millions of people, and that this could be the beginning of a whole new career for me as a director of pop videos.

'I'm not sure that I *want* a career directing pop videos,' I said. 'I want to do something meaningful, like make undercover documentaries exposing crime and corruption. Or award-winning nature programmes. And one day, feature films. I'm not sure pop videos are really my thing. And anyway, someone sitting on a chair playing the guitar hardly counts as a pop video, even with little birds and love hearts and butterflies . . .'

'Stop being such a dork.' All the time I was talking, Dodi was fiddling with the computer. 'All done,' she said when I finished explaining. 'At the very least it will make him and Flora realise how much they fancy each other.'

'Flora will kill me,' I said. 'Zach will kill me. *Zoran* will kill me.'

'Not when Zach sweeps her off her feet and declares his undying love, they won't. Then Flora and Zach will be eternally grateful, and Zoran will actually thank you, because Zach will stop being so tragic.'

That is Dodi's point of view.

Me, I just hope Flora never, ever sees it.

Tuesday 26 November

Mum and Dad left home together early this morning. I was brushing my teeth at the bathroom window and I watched as they got into the car and then just sat there, side by side in the front seats, talking for ages but not looking at each other. Even when Dad leaned over and kissed Mum on the cheek she just carried on staring out of the window, and I'm pretty sure she was crying.

'They've gone to the doctor,' said Jas on the walk to school. 'I looked in her diary.'

'But why has Dad gone with her?' I asked. Jas shrugged and said the diary didn't say why.

'It can't be serious,' Flora said. 'Dad would be nicer to her if it was.'

'I saw him kiss her,' I reminded her.

'Well, that makes a pleasant change.' Flora never worries about *anything* unless she absolutely has to.

Film club was cancelled after school today, so I came home early. The house was dark when I got back and at first I thought that it was empty, but when I went to the kitchen to make some tea the back door was open and Mum was sitting on the veranda, wrapped in a blanket and staring at the garden. I called out to her and she jumped. When she turned round I saw that she was holding a photograph.

'What are you doing?' I asked her, and she said, 'Nothing!' with that smile we all hate because it is so fake. She moved over on the sun lounger to make room for me to sit down. The photograph fell off her lap. It was a picture of Iris.

'Oh,' I said, and after that we sat very still and silent. The kettle boiled and I got up to make us both some tea. When I got back the photograph was gone and Mum had that look people get when they were about to cry but then managed to stop themselves. She took the mug I offered her. I sat on the floor with my back to her chair, and we both watched the garden, which at this time of year is basically muddy and brown except for a few roses still clinging on like nobody's told them yet that it's nearly winter.

'Something momentous is happening,' Mum said.

I thought of the photograph, and of Iris, and of this morning's secret doctor's appointment.

'Are you going to die?' I tried not to let my voice shake. Mum smiled and kissed me.

'I'm not planning on it,' she said.

'She's not *planning* on it?' Jas cried this evening when I told her. 'What does that even mean?'

I said I didn't have a clue.

'What if Flora's wrong?' Jas asked. 'What if it *is* serious?'

'I'm sure it isn't,' I said, but I am not like Flora,

and neither is Jas. If something is wrong, we would rather know about it.

My video has had thousands of hits! I can't give an exact number because people keep on looking at it, but Dodi is beside herself with excitement and I would be too if so many people weren't furious with me.

What happened was this: on Monday night, a girl in Tennessee with about a million followers on Twitter tweeted about it, posting a link to the video.

A whole bunch of her followers retweeted it.

A girl Flora used to know, who goes to Zach's school, read the tweet, saw the video and posted it to Facebook and Instagram, then retweeted it and texted and emailed the link to everyone in her address book, including Flora's best friend Tamsin. By morning break, pretty much everybody in both schools had seen it.

Flora has not responded well to global celebrity.

U. Hve. Ruined. My. Life.

That was her immediate reaction on discovering she was famous. She sent it via text ten minutes into first period, just after Tamsin showed her the video on her iPhone.

I am litrly gonna mrder u. Flora is the world's fastest texter. *I will nvr forgive u.*

'Ignore her,' Dodi whispered when I showed her my phone under the desk.

Every1 is laughing at me. Graham keeps singing at me. I am going 2 tear u lmb from lmb.

'Can I come and live with you for a bit?' I whispered back to Dodi.

U r no lnger my sister! Once I hve kld u I am nvr, evr gonna spk 2 u again. Prepare for yrs of misry.

That's when Mme Gilbert confiscated my phone. Which, quite frankly, was a relief.

Zach's response to his new-found fame has been to get into a fight. A load of people in his class were teasing him and when they didn't stop he threw a punch at one of them, and then a whole bunch of boys got involved until their teacher came in. Someone in his class filmed the whole thing and posted that on Facebook as well. It got taken down later, but not before everyone was talking about it. Zach got sent home and has been suspended till the end of the week, and Zoran is even more furious with me than Flora is. In fact he came round this afternoon just to shout at me.

'I asked you to delete that scene!' he yelled. 'Not post it all over the internet like some dating agency advert!'

I said I was really, really sorry.

'You knew how much that concert meant to him, Blue. He poured his heart and soul into that song, and then you . . .'

'I'm *sorry*,' I said again.

'And now he's in trouble at school. I had to go in this afternoon to make all sorts of excuses for him about extenuating circumstances. His *sick grandfather*. His *missing mother*. And you make fun of him!'

I started to cry. Zoran sighed and sat down next to me on the bed.

'You have so much talent,' he said quietly. 'It makes me mad to see you waste it.'

'It was Dodi's idea,' I sniffed.

'You have your own way of looking at the world, Blue. You see things other people don't. That's why you like filming, and writing. You pick up on things. You don't need to hide behind people like Dodi.'

'Dodi's fun,' I said.

'And you are serious.'

'I don't want to be *serious*.'

'Serious people can do great things.' He nudged

me with his elbow and pulled a sad, serious face. 'Stop to think before you do something like this again, OK?'

I looked at my films again after he'd gone. Mum and Flora laughing together at the bathroom window, Alina and Peter holding hands at the concert, Jas in the garden draped in kittens – is this what Zoran means about picking up on things? Because if I posted those on YouTube, I bet they wouldn't get viewed by thousands. For a moment, I felt annoyed with Zoran, because it feels like quite something to have so many people looking at what I've done. Then Jake sent me a message on Facebook to tell me Tom had sent him the link to my video and all his family were laughing their heads off about it in Australia, and I immediately felt bad again.

'It's not funny,' I wrote back.

Jake wrote, 'lol.'

I wrote that I didn't think he understood the seriousness of the situation, and when was he coming home anyway?

Jake wrote, 'Sunday,' and man, he didn't want to leave because Australia was so awesome.

I didn't reply.

The atmosphere at home is horrible, and this time it's all my fault.

'The most logical thing', Dodi said today, 'is to get Zach and Flora together.'

'In what way is that remotely logical?' I asked.

We were in our kitchen after school, eating Twig's latest batch of banana and chocolate chip cookies.

'It's what we planned to do all along,' Dodi said. 'It makes Zach happy, it makes Flora happy, it makes Zoran happy, plus now it lets you off the hook. It's the perfect solution.'

'But how?'

'We finish what we started!' Dodi cried.

'*How?*' I repeated, and Dodi admitted she didn't know.

'Think!' she ordered. We sat there for ages, munching and thinking. We finished the banana and chocolate cookies, and moved on to jam and coconut, until we eventually came up with this:

1. Stalk Zach.
2. Establish his routine.

3. Take Flora to a place their paths will cross.
4. Run away.

Which is rubbish, I pointed out to Dodi, for loads of reasons but mainly because even if we do manage to work out where Zach is going to be, Flora is about as likely to follow us there as she is to crush a kitten with her bare hands.

'We need help,' concluded Dodi. 'But who?'

We stared out at the garden. Twig had finally convinced Dad to help him build a tree house in the garden, but Dad had already given up, so now Twig and Jas were out there together, trying to finish it on their own and yelling at each other.

'There's our answer,' Dodi said.

'You only talk to us when you need something,' Jas said when we told her what we wanted her to do. 'It's rude.'

'You could pay us,' Twig suggested.

'You are obsessed with money,' I told him. Twig shrugged and said to blame the parents and their imminent separation. He said it's a well-known fact families are poorer when they divorce.

'Don't you want Flora to be happy?' asked Dodi.

'Not particularly,' said Jas, but money did it in the end.

Our plan is for Jas and Twig to beg Flora to take them shopping. They will go to the bookshop next to the record shop where Zach works on Saturdays (I don't *think* Flora knows he works there), and then Twig will say how bored he is and drag them in to look at records. If Flora says no, Jas will cry. They will go just before closing time and engage Zach in conversation, whereupon, struck with love, he will engage Flora in conversation and hopefully ask her out. Just to be sure she isn't attacked by pangs of conscience about abandoning Jas and Twig, Dodi and I (alerted by Twig, by text, on Dodi's phone) will coincidentally appear and whisk them away.

'What if he is too embarrassed to talk to her?' Jas asked.

'I would be, after that video,' Twig sniggered.

'Everything will work out just fine,' I said firmly.

Twig says he has never heard of a plan with so much potential for failure, but it hasn't stopped him taking my money. Operation Flora is costing me £5 a head for him and Jas, plus expenses, 'in case we have to buy anything while we are out'.

Things started to go wrong from the beginning, when Flora refused to take the Babes shopping, claiming excessive fame.

'I can never show my face in public again,' Flora said. 'It's all Blue's fault. She can take you.'

'I have homework,' I said.

'Surely,' Flora said, 'they are old enough to go on their own.'

'I am very, very young,' said Jas. 'And Twig is extremely irresponsible.'

'I'll take you,' said Mum from the sofa where she was lying, and we all jumped because we'd thought she was asleep.

'You mustn't!' I cried. Mum looked startled. 'You're so tired,' I said. 'And you don't look well.'

'I do feel a little sick,' she admitted.

My heart dropped. Jas and I looked at each other. Mum still hasn't told us why she went to the doctor's and neither of us has had the courage to ask.

'Oh for goodness' sake,' sighed Flora. 'Just let me find my biggest hat and sunglasses.'

Dodi and I followed them at a discreet distance. We stopped just inside the park, out of sight but close enough to the shops to get there within minutes of Twig texting us.

Later, Twig told me exactly what happened. The plan carried on going wrong when instead of heading straight to the bookshop, like she was supposed to, Flora dived into a clothes shop then bumped into Tamsin, who suggested they go for coffee. Jas dragged her away but when they finally got to the record shop, Zach wasn't there.

'He left early,' Twig texted.

'Well where the ****** **** is he then?' I said to Dodi.

'Over there,' she replied.

Right in front of us, across the lawn on the basketball courts. Shooting hoops and looking moody, all on his own.

After that, things moved very fast.

I texted Twig back to tell him where we were.

Jas announced that vinyl records were a waste of time, especially since we don't have a record player, and that she wanted to go to the park.

Flora, who was enjoying herself, said tough.

Jas ran away.

Flora ran after her.

Twig, after a quick text to me, followed.

'They will be here in about two minutes,' I informed Dodi.

'Which will be too late!' she hissed. 'He's leaving!'

It was true. Zach had tucked his basketball under his arm and was lolloping – I swear, he lollops – away from us across the court.

Dodi grabbed my hand.

'Come on!' she cried, and started running.

So there we were. Flora, Jas and Twig running down the high street. Dodi and me tearing after Zach. Zach, unaware of any of us, lolloping.

'How are we going to stop him?' I panted.

'Leave it to me,' she gasped.

We drew level with Zach. Dodi threw herself at his feet.

'I'm sorry!' she cried. 'We weren't laughing at you! We never thought so many people would watch the video!'

Zach just stared at her.

'Forgive us!' Dodi begged.

'Dodi.' I nodded towards the park entrance. Jas and Twig were streaking across the lawn towards us, trailed by Flora.

'We have to go!' Dodi shouted. And then Dodi and I ran away, except we were laughing so much we had to run with our legs crossed so as not to pee.

Zach just carried on staring. He stared as we vanished down the path and dived into a bush, and he stared some more as Jas and Twig shot past and followed us, and then he stared and stared and stared as Flora, red and breathless and still wearing her hat and sunglasses, erupted on to the court, screeched to a halt and stared back.

The four of us huddled together in the bushes and watched.

'This plan was catastrophic,' I said.

'I did warn you,' said Twig.

'They're talking!' cried Jas.

She was right. We were too far away to hear what they were saying, but they were *definitely* talking. Flora and Zach, face to face on the basketball court. He shuffled his feet, tossing his ball from one hand to the other. She fiddled with her earring. He pointed down the path to where we were hiding. Flora turned as if to go. Zach put his hand out, like he was asking her to stay. And she did.

'Bingo,' whispered Dodi.

'Time to go home,' I agreed.

We crept out of the bushes and went the long way round the park so as not to disturb them.

It was almost dark by the time Flora got home. She didn't mention the fact that Twig and Jas had run away, and nobody asked her where she'd been. But tonight I heard her humming Zach's song to herself in the bathroom, and I think that tomorrow she may start talking to me again.

Sunday 1 December (very early in the morning)

Tomorrow, or rather today, started almost before yesterday ended and Flora is already talking to me. I had been asleep about five minutes when something landed on the end of my bed, and when I opened my eyes that something was her.

'Are you awake?' she whispered.

'No,' I mumbled.

'So I met Zach.'

Flora giggled, and stretched out at the end of my bed with her feet dangling over one side and her head hanging down over the other.

Before today, I never really thought much about love at first sight. It's just one of those things you assume must be true because films and books are always going on about it, but Flora is my first real-life experience of it, and it's extremely strange. She's had about a million crushes and boyfriends before, but this is the first time she has come into my bedroom in the middle of the night to talk about it.

'He's so gorgeous,' she said. 'I mean, close up. He's got these amazing brown eyes, and when he smiles his mouth goes up a little bit more one side than the other, which is adorable, and he has a dimple in his left cheek. And he's really funny. I apologised about you and your video. I mentioned, you know, the fight thing, and he got all embarrassed and said he didn't normally go around punching people. He said that song was very personal to him, and it upset him seeing it taken apart like that. He's so sensitive and artistic. He said he had a lot on his mind, and I said I knew a bit about it through Zoran, but discreetly, you know, like I didn't mention his witch mother not coming to the concert or anything. I just said very vaguely about his grandfather and how I was sorry, and he was all yeah, well, it was tough but he didn't want to talk about it and then it was a tiny bit awkward but he asked if he could see me again!'

'Your face is going red,' I said. 'I think the blood must be going to your head.'

Flora flipped back the right way up and beamed at me.

'Did I tell you he smells delicious? Like lemons. Or maybe limes.'

'That's so lovely.'

'I'm going back to bed now.'

She glided over to the door in a sort of weird improvised ballet and drifted out.

I have been lying awake for ages. Jake comes home today. I realise that I have absolutely no idea what he smells like.

Sunday 1 December (continued)

If I was making a film about me and Jake, I would call it something like *The Saga of Bluebell and Jake*, and it would go like this:

The Saga of Bluebell and Jake

The Day He Came Home

BLUE, looking casually elegant without her glasses, sits on a park bench

gazing wistfully at the duck pond.
JAKE appears soundlessly behind her.

                    JAKE
        You are even more beautiful than I
                  remembered.

Blue turns towards him with a dainty
sob. Jake folds her in his manly arms.

                    BLUE
         Jake! How delicious! You smell
          exactly like cinnamon toast!

Or this: BLUE walks down the street
with a group of friends, carefree and
laughing, when they run into JAKE
hurrying towards them, carrying a
bunch of flowers and a haunted
expression.

                    JAKE
         (his voice choked with emotion)
         Thank God you're alive! I've been
        trying to call you every day since

                     74

your last witty and amusing email, to
apologise for sharing it with my
entire family!

BLUE
Mme Gilbert confiscated my phone!

JAKE
(folding her in his manly arms)
Your eyes are like the ocean on a
summer's day and your fragrance
reminds me of roses.

I know both of these would be super cheesy, but I still think they would be better than what actually did happen today, which was – nothing.

I waited all day for Jake to call. I don't even know why I got so worked up about it. Maybe it was Flora last night, like all that head-over-heels stuff was contagious. Maybe I do like him more than I thought. Or maybe it was just Dodi, turning up at the crack of dawn with her hair curlers and a bag full of make-up, making me feel like it was all a much bigger deal than it was.

'You have to be dazzling,' she scolded when I tried

to resist her makeover. She made me steam and exfoliate my face, then started to turn my dead-straight hair into droopy ringlets.

'They're pretty and feminine,' she said.

'They're hideous,' I retorted, but Dodi said I had to trust her.

'I'm going to leave you the make-up and the curlers,' she said, after painting my nails pink and showing me how to make up my eyes. 'Make sure you get up early tomorrow morning to use them. And if Jake comes round, put on just a tiny bit of lipgloss. You don't want him to think you're trying too hard.'

'My hair is *curly*,' I said, but she said that was different.

The more he didn't call, the more I wished he would. After Dodi had gone, I sat down at my desk and did my homework. I worked all afternoon and I tried not to jump every time I heard a telephone or the doorbell ring, and when Dodi called this evening for an update I pretended I didn't care, but I do. At least, I *think* I do.

If I wish Jake would call me, it means I really like him – doesn't it?

If Iris were here, she would laugh at the lot of us – Dodi being bossy and Jake's rubbish emails and me being so nervous. Even though she died way before any of us were into boys, I know she would have made me feel better. It's December today. For most people that means Christmas and holidays, but for me it's the month when she died, and right now the only thing I'm absolutely certain about is how much I miss her.

Monday 2 December

Dodi gave me precise instructions about what to wear today, but I overslept, and then I realised all my tights have holes in them so I couldn't wear my new puffball skirt like she said I should, and my jeans were all in the wash so all I had were some old dungarees that make me look as though I'm about nine years old. Flora said I looked like an extra on a farming programme but by then it was gone eight and I had to run to get to school on time.

Dodi looked disapproving as I slid in next to her in assembly. 'You're red,' she said. 'You haven't done your hair and you're not wearing any make-up. Also, you're sweating.'

'Is he here?' I panted.

'Two rows down, right at the end,' she sighed. 'And what's with the farm girl look?'

'It's only Jake,' I said, but my heart was hammering. From where I was sitting, I could just see the back of his head. Tom and Colin were jostling him. Jake turned round and smiled this little smile, and I saw that he was looking very brown and fit from his holiday. I admit that was not what I was expecting. In my mind he was still what he always was before he went away, which was more pale and interesting.

'Only Jake,' Dodi smirked.

Dodi says that Jake has come home hot. I don't know how I feel about this. It's difficult enough coming to terms with the whole idea of having a boyfriend at all, let alone a hot one, and I think Jake is maybe a bit confused too. He bought me a bush hat with corks hanging from it and a boomerang, which is nice but hardly romantic. Then later, when we were walking home with the others, he barely said a word. I thought that maybe we would stop in the park or he would ask me over to his place, like he used to do sometimes when we were just friends, but when we reached our usual crossroads all he said was 'See you tomorrow, Blue,' and we went our separate ways.

I think this may all be a giant mistake.

I ran into Flora on the way home. She and Zach both had free periods this afternoon, and she was all aglow with love after meeting up with him at Home Sweet Home. Jas was sitting on her own in the kitchen when we got in, surrounded by notebooks, and I think she found Flora as irritating as I do because she took one look at her and grumbled that her whole family was obsessed with romance.

'Grumpy!' Flora carolled. 'Where's Twig?'

Twig, Jas informed us, had gone straight from school to the railway bridge by the canal, to look at the trains passing underneath.

'Maisie Carter has a little brother,' she spat. 'Maisie's little brother likes trains. Maisie was supposed to look after him after school today but she had better things to do, so she asked Twig to take him to look at the choo-choos.'

'That's so sweet,' said Flora.

Jas said she thought it was revolting.

Wednesday 4 December

Dodi says that Jake isn't behaving like a proper boyfriend should. He doesn't wait for me after lessons or talk to me on my own or behave like anything between us is at all different. She thinks he's trying to avoid me. Like today there was only him and me and Dodi at lunch, because Tom and Colin had a detention, and Dodi said, trying to leave us alone, 'I have to go to the library now to research population density in the Sahara,' and instead of staying with me he said he had homework to do too, and we all ended up going together.

'It's not what you want in a boyfriend,' Dodi said. She says she is going to talk to him and explain the basic rules of going out with people.

I told her what I thought about it all being a giant mistake.

'I think actually we may not be going out any more and he just hasn't told me,' I said.

'Holding hands,' Dodi went on, not listening to me again. 'Going on dates. Spending time together. *Kissing.*'

'I'm not sure I'm ready for any of those things,' I said, but Dodi says of course I am.

The Saga of Bluebell and Jake

The Kiss
Or, Utter Humiliation

EXTERIOR. DAY.

JAKE and BLUE walk home along a London
street in awkward silence.

> JAKE
> (staring at the pavement)
> So, d'you want to go to the cinema
> or something?

> BLUE
> (examining the bark of a tree)
> I, um, er, gah.

> JAKE
> (apparently not noticing that Blue is
> dying, strangled by her own embarrassment)
> Saturday afternoon?

                    BLUE
            Hem, er, goo, agh.

                    JAKE
        Right, well, see you tomorrow then.

He pounces and presses his mouth
against hers. She makes a choking
sound and runs away.

And that was it. My first proper kiss.

I don't know what Dodi said to Jake, but we were all hanging around outside the sweet shop together after school when the others just *vanished*, and the whole pounce/kiss/running away thing happened.

The film of my life is not even a tragedy. A tragedy is *Romeo and Juliet* or *Titanic*, where everybody dies. My life is barely even a rom-com. At best, it's reality TV, except sometimes it doesn't even feel real.

'What's it like when you kiss Zach?' I asked Flora when she breezed in this evening.

'Like it's none of your business,' she replied.

'But really.'

And Flora is truly in an exceptionally good mood at the moment because instead of saying what I fully expected, which was 'I don't have time to instruct inferior sisters in the art of love,' she went all dreamy.

'Magic,' she sighed. 'Like we're the only two people in the whole world, and everything is still, like time has stopped but is spinning really fast at the same time. And warm. Like coming home. Like there's nowhere else I ever want to be.' She was sort of staring into space, but then she gave herself a little 'ah well, back to the real world' shake and said, 'Why, what's it like with Jake?'

'We're not really into that sort of thing,' I said.

'What, like *kissing*?' she said, and then thank God Jas came into my room and said, 'Can I ask you something?'

'You're covered in ink,' Flora said as she left. 'I swear I never worked that hard in primary school.'

Jas ignored her. 'I need you to help me,' she told me. I said the last time she asked me to help her we all ended up combing our hair for fleas.

'I'm not in the mood,' I told Jas. 'I am thinking important thoughts, and I need to write them down.'

Kissing Jake did not feel remotely like coming home.

Kissing Jake felt wet and odd, and not at all how a first kiss ought to.

Friday 6 December

Today before going to work Mum put all the laundry in the bin instead of the washing machine. She realised what she'd done when she came home

84

this afternoon, and sat down in the middle of the kitchen floor and cried. Then Dad came in to find out what all the noise was and sat right down on the floor beside her.

'I didn't like those shirts anyway,' he said. Mum started to laugh and threw her arms around his neck, and then they went to bed. We haven't seen them since, except when Dad came down to make cheese on toast because Mum was hungry. He got a text while he was making it, and it was from Mum in the bedroom telling him she wanted Rice Krispies as well. I haven't seen him laugh so much *ever*. I didn't even know Mum liked Rice Krispies.

Saturday 7 December

Zach was working today, so Flora couldn't go and see him, but apparently if she isn't with him she has to talk about him *all the time*. She hardly stopped all day.

'He hasn't seen his mother for *over two years*,' she told us. 'You know I used to think she was a witch? Well, it turns out nice Mr Rudowski threw her out after Zach's grandma died and told her to never come back. Zach's never forgiven him for it.'

'That sounds very dramatic,' Mum said. She was tired again. Jas and I were sitting on her bed playing cards with her to keep her company, while Flora went on about Zach and Twig practised hairstyles in the bathroom.

'It's true!' Flora insisted. 'Zach says she was a brilliant mum. She used to do things like take him out of school to go to the seaside, or camp overnight in Richmond Park. One time she took him for tea at the Ritz and wore a long gold cocktail dress and made him pretend she was the queen of Narnia.'

'She sounds funny,' Jas said, shuffling cards. 'Why don't you ever do anything like that, Mummy?'

'She sounds weird,' I said. 'And if she's so brilliant, how come she isn't here now?'

'She lives in the South of France now. Zach really, really wanted her to come to his concert, and she wrote and told him she would try, but he thinks she didn't come because she's so scared of his grandfather.'

'His grandfather who's in hospital?' I said.

Flora said she didn't see what difference that made, and why were her family always so unsupportive when she tried to tell them things, and then Dad came in and said, 'Personally, I'm a little worried about this young man.'

86

'Were you *listening*?' Jas looked impressed. 'Like *spying*?'

Dad said he'd seen the video of Zach fighting in his classroom and he didn't like it. Flora said, 'Oh my God, you *are* spying on me,' and Dad said that's what happens when you let your parents friend you on Facebook.

'I don't believe this!' Flora cried.

'I don't like boyfriends,' Dad said. 'They disturb things.'

'Like kittens?' Mum said. They looked at each other and once again I got the feeling that they were talking about something else completely.

'Ignore your father,' Mum said. 'He's just trying to provoke you.'

'No I'm not,' Dad said. 'I am trying to *protect* her.'

'That fight was completely out of character,' Flora insisted. 'He was upset.'

Mum said she was absolutely certain Zach was a very nice boy, and she hoped he would come to the house one day so she could meet him. Flora said that would probably scare him off for good.

'He's not used to this sort of thing.' She waved at Mum and Jas and me all piled on the bed, with Dad lounging in a chair with his feet up on the bedside table.

'I don't think your mother was planning on receiving him in her *bedroom*,' Dad said, and Flora swept out, saying he was impossible, and pretending not to notice that everyone was laughing at her.

'How is Jake?' Mum asked me, to change the subject.

'Forget about Jake!' Flora cried from the landing. 'They haven't even *kissed* yet!'

'I'm glad to hear it!' Dad roared back at her.

If you could die from blushing, I would be stone cold dead.

'Actually,' I muttered, 'I have a date with him this afternoon.'

'That's wonderful!' Mum patted my hand. 'And you mustn't worry about the kissing,' she yawned. 'There's plenty of time for that.'

And just like that, she fell asleep. Jas and I stared at her, amazed.

'Do you think she's all right?' Jas whispered.

'She looks quite peaceful,' I whispered back.

'*Plenty of time for kissing*,' Jas smirked.

'Shut up,' I said.

Flora is so right not to want Zach to meet our family.

I couldn't bring myself to write about my date with Jake yesterday. It was sort of – hurtful. I stayed in my room all of Sunday, and thought about not going to school at all today, except unlike Zach's mother Mum doesn't believe in people missing school unless they are ill.

Dodi pounced on me straight after registration, having already heard the most essential details.

'Tom and Colin went too?' she cried. 'I don't believe it!'

'How did you know?' I asked.

'Cressida saw you in the queue. She couldn't believe it either. She says you went to see *X-Men*!'

'I happen to like *X-Men*,' I lied. I couldn't tell her the truth, either about the film or about the fact that Jake hardly talked to me the whole evening.

Dodi said that the point wasn't whether I liked it or not, the point was it just wasn't the sort of film you took someone to on a first date, with or without a posse of your best friends.

'I can't believe Cressida is gossiping about me,' I said.

'The problem is that you're too familiar,' Dodi said. 'Jake sees you too much as a friend.'

'The problem', I corrected her, 'is that he obviously doesn't want to go out with me any more.'

'You have to make yourself more alluring,' Dodi decided.

'How?' I asked.

'More seductive.'

'HOW?' I repeated.

'Pout, or flutter your eyelashes or something. Maybe giggle when he talks to you. Put on some more lipgloss. I haven't seen you wear make-up once since your makeover.'

'Lipgloss makes my lips sticky,' I said. 'And I refuse to giggle. Flora does it all the time with Zach and it's really annoying.'

Dodi rolled her eyes like I was the annoying one.

'Smile,' she ordered.

I grinned, baring my teeth.

'Not at me!' she screeched. 'At him! And *nicely*! Take off your glasses.'

I put my glasses in my pocket and smiled more softly.

'Good,' said Dodi. 'You know, you really are so pretty when you try. And now I'm going to talk to Jake again.'

'I'd really rather you didn't,' I told her, but she was already gone.

The Saga of Bluebell and Jake

The Kiss (take 2)

BLUE, accompanied by DODI, comes out of the school gate. JAKE is waiting on the pavement. Dodi nudges Blue, who removes her glasses. She is wearing lipgloss. Jake leaves TOM and COLIN and marches up to her, looking determined and still a little bit tanned and therefore quite handsome.

                    JAKE
    (sounding as determined as he looks)
            Walk you home?

                    BLUE
    (beaming, trying not to look like
    this whole episode isn't mortifying)
            Why thank you, kind sir.

Together, they head off parkwards. Blue steals a glance over her shoulder. Dodi pouts and blows kisses. Colin and Tom see her and snigger. Jake ignores them. Blue carries on beaming despite aching cheek muscles.

                    JAKE
          Shall we sit on this bench?

                    BLUE
          That would be lovely.

They stop at a park bench. For a while, they sit side by side in silence. Then Jake turns towards Blue. Blue, still manically grinning, turns towards Jake. Jake clears his throat, leans forwards and kisses Blue on the mouth. Blue, resisting the very real urge to giggle, kisses him back. Jake closes his eyes. She closes hers.

I tried to avoid Jake for most of the week. It was all I wanted to do, after that date. All I could think was that if he didn't see me, he wouldn't be able to dump me. Being dumped by Jake would just be the most humiliating thing in the world.

By sliding into lessons at the last minute, eating lunch in the library and hiding in the girls' loos at the end of the day, I managed not to speak to him for days, but there's no escaping Dodi when she's on a mission.

Flora, who heard about the disastrous film date from Cressida's older sister, said I should be the one dumping Jake, not running scared that he was going to dump me. I told her, 'If I dump him, it will show he upset me, and that would be embarrassing too,' and she said that was stupid but I'm really, really glad now that I didn't listen to her, just like I'm really glad Dodi's my best friend.

The Earth didn't spin the second time Jake kissed me, but it was a lot better.

In fact it was quite nice.

I'm not sure I can write about it right now. I'm feeling a little bit giddy.

Today I had to take Jas to her riding lesson. This is something Dad normally does, but apparently he has reached another critical point in his novel and cannot be interrupted whatever the circumstances.

Riding lessons were Jas's birthday present from Grandma before she left for Arizona. Grandma, who is horse mad, almost wept when Jas asked for them in the summer. She even rang Jas up from the ranch where she is staying on the first night of her holiday to rant about GALLOPING ON THE WIDE OPEN PLAINS and THE BEAUTY OF SIMPLE HONEST HORSE FOLK and how happy she was that she and Jas might one day be SHARING THIS TOGETHER.

The stables where Jas goes are right beneath the motorway, a tiny yard sandwiched between a bus depot and a leisure centre. They are about as far from the wide open plains as it is possible to get, but I can see why Jas loves them. It *is* rather incredible, after walking from the Tube down an alleyway covered in graffiti, to stumble on a lot of plump, glossy ponies. Jas skipped into the yard like she owned the place and ran up to greet a young woman who was striding around the yard in skin-tight jodhpurs and knee-high riding boots, cracking a whip and barking orders at about half a dozen children who were scurrying around with saddles.

'This is Gloria,' Jas announced. 'Gloria, this is my sister Blue.'

'Very pleased to meet you,' Gloria said. 'You can help Jas tack up Mopsy.'

I followed Jas into the tack room, where an old man who looked like a tramp sat drinking tea.

'That's Bill,' Jas whispered. 'He's Gloria's father. He used to be a jockey.'

Bill looked like he could barely walk, let alone ride a horse. I waved at him. He grunted. Jas reached behind him to pick up a bridle.

'Not that one,' he snapped.

If anyone at home ever spoke to Jas like that, she would probably burst into tears, but here she just laughed, picked up a different bridle and skipped out again to tack up her pony. The old man watched her go, and I swear I thought he might be smiling, but when he saw me watching he went straight back to being grumpy.

The lesson was a typical riding lesson, lots of girls and one boy following each other nose to tail round the ring, with Gloria shouting instructions at them through a loudspeaker. I watched Jas bounce round an obstacle course. Her pony knocked over two traffic cones and a tub of plastic geraniums. Gloria made her do it again. Crouched over the pony's neck, her black hair falling about her face and her cheeks flushed, Jas was like a different person, happy and confident and like she could take on anything. It was strange, looking at her. It made me wonder if this was the real Jas, as she was meant to be, as opposed to the Jas we see every day, who cries and worries and gets cross. It felt almost like I didn't know her. And then that made me think about how well we know anybody, including ourselves.

Jake's family have friends over from Australia this weekend, which means I can't see him. I asked him if he couldn't sneak away, just for a little bit, but he said no and he would see me at school on Monday.

Monday feels like an awfully long way away. I think I do like Jake now.

I can't believe I have a proper boyfriend!

Mum came into my room tonight after I had gone to bed. She hasn't done that for ages. I thought, maybe mothers have a sort of instinct about these things and she has come to talk to me about Jake, but she didn't say anything at all for a really long time. She didn't get into bed with me either, like she used to, but instead sat on my window seat, looking out at the garden even though it was completely dark.

'We'll have to get a Christmas tree soon,' she said at last.

I got a lump in my throat then, because I thought I knew what was troubling her. Christmas trees are always difficult in our family, because they always remind us of Iris.

'It'll be OK,' I said.

'Will it?' she asked. She looked like she often looks these days, like she's about to cry, and I finally screwed up the courage to ask what I haven't asked since she had that secret appointment with the doctor.

'Mum, are you sure you're OK?' I asked.

'What do you mean?'

'You seem so sad.'

'I'm always sad at this time of year.'

'Apart from that.'

'There is nothing to worry about,' Mum said, and I know I should have been nice, but I'm really tired of her secrets. So instead I said that if there was nothing else she needed could she please get out of my room because I wanted to go to sleep.

'Don't be cross,' she said.

'Don't be annoying,' I replied.

She left, like I asked, but then I wished she hadn't. I'm not quite sure how you do tell your mum about your boyfriend, but I think it might have been nice to talk to her about Jake. And we used to have this thing in our family, before Iris died, where nobody was allowed to go to bed angry or sad, but that clearly doesn't apply any more.

The Film Diaries of Bluebell Gadsby

Scene Five
The Dinner Party

INTERIOR. NIGHT.

Once again, we are in the Gadsby family
kitchen, with MOTHER at the cooking
range, this time doing something
complicated with prunes. A leg of lamb
rests on top of the stove, and an apple
tart sits on the side, next to a bowl
of custard.

FATHER lays the table. Under strict
instructions, he takes unusual care
over this, putting out candles and
silverware and the tablecloth
inherited from Mother's grandmother,
vintage linen with lace trimmings.
JASMINE sits on the sofa with her nose
in a book and the kittens in her lap.

Father places plates of smoked salmon
on the table.

FATHER
(irritable)
It would be nice if at least one of
my daughters helped me.

MOTHER
(oddly soothing)
Don't be cross, darling. I asked
Blue to film this. I thought it would
be nice. Jas, give your father a
hand.

Jasmine sighs and peels herself off
the sofa. The kittens (now over four
months old and no longer tiny) start
to pad around the room.

JASMINE
(taking in extent of food spread for
the first time)
Is anyone coming for dinner?

MOTHER
(sounding nervous)

No darling, just us. Your father and
I . . .

                    FATHER
                  (warning)
                  Cassie!

                    FLORA
          (bursting into the kitchen)
        He's here! He's nearly here! Is
              everything ready?
        (taking in the table, the napkins,
              the roast lamb)
        What are you doing? He'll be
        terrified! I said it would just be
                    pasta!

                    FATHER
        What on earth are you talking about?

                    FLORA
        Zach! I asked him and Zoran for
        dinner. Mum, didn't you get my text?

                    MOTHER
              (looking appalled)
        My phone's out of battery.

                    FATHER
               (looking furious)
          Call him right now and tell him he
                  can't come!

                    FLORA
          Oh my God, what is *wrong* with you?

TWIG enters in his underpants. Flora
screams at him to put some clothes on.
Twig replies that he doesn't have any
clothes because Mother accidentally
donated all his jeans to charity.
Mother replies he should stop
complaining about his clothes being
too small. Twig answers that normal
people buy replacement clothes *before*
giving the old ones away. Flora
declares there is no way she is letting
her boyfriend see her brother naked.
Hermione quietly hops on to the table
and starts to eat the smoked salmon.
Father bats her away, knocking over a
bottle of red wine.

MOTHER

My grandmother's tablecloth!

FATHER

(roaring)

TO HELL WITH THE TABLECLOTH! AND TO
HELL WITH CATS, AND CANDLES, AND
INCONVENIENT BOYFRIENDS! TO HELL WITH
ALL THE THINGS CONSTANTLY CONSPIRING
TO DISRUPT EVERYTHING I TRY TO DO!

The whole family stares at him,
fascinated. Nobody but CAMERAMAN
(Blue) notices the kitchen door open,
revealing a worried-looking ZORAN and
a frankly petrified-looking ZACH.

MOTHER

David, calm down.

FATHER

THIS IS NOT WHAT THIS EVENING WAS
MEANT TO BE ABOUT!

ZORAN

(very softly)

What was it meant to be about, David?

Father slumps, looking defeated and almost as terrified as Zach. Mother goes to him, takes his hand, then turns to face the camera.

                    MOTHER
        We're going to have a baby.

Poor Zach. I bet he thought the first time he met Flora's family it would be all about him. He probably rehearsed it in front of the mirror in Zoran's tiny bathroom, wondering if he should call Dad *sir* or *Mr Gadsby*, and was it all right to wear a hoody or should he wear a shirt and should he buy Mum flowers or stuff like that. I bet he had no idea he was going to stumble into a room full of flying kittens and a load of people screaming and crying because they'd just heard life-changing news, straight after hearing himself described as *inconvenient*. I bet that was the last thing he expected.

'This is not unusual behaviour,' I heard Zoran reassure Zach as they stood in the doorway, and then he was sweeping into the room and hugging Mum.

'You told them at last!' he said.

'You knew!' I cried.

'I've been begging him to come back when the baby is born,' Mum sniffed. 'And I was so worried how you all would take the news, with the age difference and everything.'

I knew that by *everything*, she meant Iris.

Apparently Zoran has been saying she should tell us for ages but she was too scared. Then when I got cross with her last night she realised she couldn't keep it secret any more.

'Are you happy?' she asked me.

'I think so,' I stammered.

'A baby!' Flora looked stunned.

'Will it be a boy?' Twig asked.

Jas didn't say anything to Mum or Dad at all. Instead she moved away from the little crowd gathered around the parents, making a beeline for Zach, looking very shy but also quite determined.

'I loved your song,' I heard her whisper to him. Zach stopped looking scared and looked embarrassed instead.

'Can I ask you a question?' she asked, and then she saw me listening and frowned for me to go away.

Dinner was nice and barely burned at all. I think Mum was so relieved her secret was finally out she couldn't stop laughing. She actually thought she couldn't have babies any more, so it took her ages to realise she was pregnant. She's known for months, but she and Dad didn't want to tell us until they were used to the idea.

'We were a bit shaken up at first,' Mum said.

I'm not sure Dad is at all used to the idea of the

baby yet. When Flora asked if they had thought of any names yet and Mum said what did we think about Hazel, either for a boy or a girl, he winced, and not just because he doesn't like the name Hazel. Talking about names, he said, made the whole thing feel more real.

'Of course it's real!' Flora cried. 'Now I know Mum's pregnant, I can see the bump and everything! I can't believe we didn't notice before!'

'It will be all right, David,' Mum beamed, and Dad gulped down more wine.

Twig, Jas and I didn't say much at all, but Flora and Zoran made up for it. Some people are like that, they can just chat away non-stop whatever is going on, as if a massive bombshell hasn't just landed on them. Zach sat next to Flora, and at first he was completely silent, but then Mum asked him how his grandfather was and about his music, and Dad started going on about how he was in a band at school and reminiscing about all the gigs he used to go to, and Flora looked like she might die of embarrassment except it turns out that Zach likes a lot of the music Dad used to like. And then Twig, who was sitting on the other side of him, started to talk to him about football, and also asked him if he was any good at carpentry, because he would like to finish building the tree house, and even though Zach didn't become exactly talkative, he stopped looking like the whole plan for the evening was to flay him alive and throw his body to a pack of ravenous vultures.

I didn't talk to him until the end of the evening, because I was building up the courage for what I had to say, but just before they left, when Zoran was hugging everyone and Zach was standing on his own, I went up to him and apologised. I didn't even try to blame it on Dodi. I'd actually rehearsed a whole speech, but in the end all I managed to mumble was 'I'm really sorry about the video,' and he blushed and mumbled back, 'Hey, don't worry about it.' I thought we were going to leave it at that but then he added, 'Actually, I looked at it again, and it's pretty funny,' and suddenly I completely got why Flora is so crazy about him. I know it's a cliché, but his whole face really does light up when he smiles, and he has this way of looking at you, like you really matter.

Zach is lovely.

The parents think so too. 'What a nice boy,' Mum said when they had gone. Dad said yes, and did she think he should take up the guitar again, and then they went up to bed hand in hand like they'd never had a fight in their whole lives. And Flora beamed and floated on upstairs after them, followed by Twig, who is pleased because in one evening he has accumulated not only a sort of brother-in-law who plays football and can build tree houses, but also potentially an actual brother.

Which just left Jas and me.

A *baby*.

I can't believe it.

A baby. Not a fatal illness or imminent death or divorce. A *baby*.

On the way to school this morning, Flora said, 'You do realise what this means, don't you, it means the parents still do it.' Jas said, 'Do what?' and Flora said, 'Well, how do you think babies are made?' Twig made a gagging noise. Jas blushed scarlet and said, 'Oh that, I know that!' and then we were silent, all thinking private thoughts about Mum and Dad making babies. It was an enormous relief when Dodi bounced up to us at the crossroads.

'What's up?' Dodi asked. 'You all look a bit sick.'

I told her, and then immediately felt guilty

because I'm sure her reaction was exactly what mine should have been.

'That's AMAZING!' Dodi shouted. 'A baby! I love babies! They're so cute!'

'They cry all night and they poo in their pants,' said Twig. 'How is that cute?'

'Oh my God!' Dodi was struck by a sudden thought and just looking at her I could tell what it was. 'That means your parents still . . .'

I felt better.

'Babies *are* cute.' Flora brightened. 'When it's born, Zach and I can take it to the park and pretend it's ours!'

Twig said that was just weird, but I wish I could be like Flora. Life must be so simple when you're her.

Dodi and I skipped assembly. Dodi pretended to have really bad cramps and I said I had to look after her, and we settled on the floor of the science block toilets, which are still pretty clean first thing in the morning.

'Are you pleased?' Dodi asked, and I told her I didn't know.

'I bet it's weird,' she said, and I said yes, it was.

'But still, nice,' said Dodi. 'And you mustn't think about Iris. It's not about her, it's not about her at all.'

That is why, however annoying she can be, I love Dodi. Because she always knows what I'm thinking.

I wanted to talk to Jake about the baby too, but he was really quiet today. 'That's so awesome,' he said when I told him, but then when I tried to explain how I was feeling about it, I could tell he wasn't really listening.

'Boys are rubbish at emotional stuff,' Dodi said to make me feel better.

'Jake never used to be,' I replied. Dodi said that she had read in a magazine that some boys find it quite hard to go from friend to boyfriend, and that I had to try and be understanding and give him time and space. So when Jake told me he couldn't walk home with me after school this afternoon, I just smiled like I really couldn't care less and said that was fine, because I couldn't walk home with him either, and then I went to meet Mum at her office.

I waited for her outside. She came out looking tired but sort of smiley, and like Flora I wondered how none of us ever even noticed how much she's changed. Now that I know she's pregnant, it seems so obvious. It's not so much that she has a big round tummy, but her whole body is so much *thicker* than it used to be. Zoran once told me that people only ever see what they want to see, and I suppose he must be right.

'Blue!' She jumped when she saw me, but I don't think she was that surprised. I said could we talk, and she tucked her arm into mine and said she knew just the place.

The church was small and dark and cold, but it smelled of incense and someone had put flowers in front of the altar. A priest in long dark robes was talking to an old lady in one of the front pews. He raised his hand at Mum and smiled like he knew her.

'I come in here sometimes at lunchtime,' Mum said. 'It's a nice place to be quiet.'

She led me to one of those tables where you can light candles and put some coins in the box.

'It's not Christmas yet,' I said.

Christmas is pretty much the only time we ever go to church, to remember Iris, who died on Christmas Eve.

Mum just handed me a candle. I tried to pray, but I'm not very good at praying, so I thought instead. I thought about how Iris would feel if it was her standing here instead of me. Iris loved baby animals, and really a human baby isn't so different from, say, a puppy or a kitten. I thought about how she would never know this baby, and how wrong that was.

'Do you want to feel it kicking?' Mum whispered, and I wasn't sure but she took my hand anyway and put it against her tummy underneath her coat. Apparently I used to always feel Twig and Jas kick when she was pregnant with them, but I can't remember it and I wasn't expecting it to feel like that, so *strong*. I jumped when the baby kicked my hand, and screamed out loud. The priest and the old lady looked up, saw what was going on and smiled.

'How do you think it feels for *me*?' Mum laughed.

'Do you already love it?' I asked. 'Like you love us?'

She took so long to answer I thought maybe she wasn't going to, but then she said that the way you love a baby is very different from the way you love an older child and that sometimes she thought she loved us all more and more as we grew up. She said nothing mattered more to her in the whole world than keeping us safe and that it still destroyed her to know she couldn't stop bad things happening to us, and did I understand?

I nodded. I couldn't speak, because I had such a big lump in my throat.

'You mustn't worry if you don't know what to make of it. It's a lot to think about. Babies upset things, as your father might say.'

'Like boyfriends,' I said. 'And kittens.'

I reached out to touch her tummy again. It felt different this time, bigger and rounder than the sharp limb which had jabbed at me earlier.

'The head,' Mum said.

'Will I hurt it?'

'It's tougher than you think.'

I don't know how long we sat there, me with my head on Mum's shoulder, her arms around me and my hand on the baby's head in her tummy. Eventually the old priest coughed and said he was sorry to disturb us but he had to close the church. Mum squeezed me tight before letting me go.

'I want us to make this the best Christmas,' she said. She didn't say 'since Iris died', but I knew what she meant. She never answered my question about loving the baby, but she didn't need to.

Wednesday 18 December

We broke up for the holidays at lunchtime. I went to Home Sweet Home with the others. Colin, Dodi and Tom were messing around trying to remember all the verses of 'Rudolph the Red-Nosed Reindeer'. I sat next to Jake, who was still being really quiet, and then when we left the cafe I hung back so I could walk with him and asked if he was OK.

Jake said that he was fine.

'You know you can talk to me about anything, right?' I said.

The others had all stopped at the little Christmas market which has been up since the beginning of December. Mostly they sell things like food and mulled wine and expensive stuff we can't afford, but one stall has an everything under £2.99 section, including a Santa badge Colin was buying for his little sister.

'It's so awesome,' he said. 'Look what happens when you press the middle.'

We looked. The badge lit up and started playing 'Jingle Bells'. We all laughed, even Jake.

He has a nice laugh.

'That's amazing,' I said, because it kind of was.

'My sister's going to love it,' Colin said.

'What are you getting Blue for Christmas, Jake?' Dodi asked.

Jake looked a bit panicked at that and said he hadn't thought about it. I said it didn't matter, I hadn't bought him anything yet either, and I was going shopping for presents on Saturday.

'But Jake's going to his gran's tomorrow,' Tom

said. 'You'd better get him something before he goes, Blue, or he might dump you.'

Dodi told Tom he was an idiot.

'I thought you weren't going to your gran's till Christmas Eve?' I said to Jake, and he went very red and said that things had changed and he was going early.

A band started playing Christmas songs, and Dodi dragged me off to look at them. The boys joined us a few minutes later. Jake was quieter than ever on the way home, but when we said goodbye in the park, he gave me my present, which was a Santa badge.

'I bought it when you were listening to the band,' he said, looking embarrassed. 'You said Colin's was amazing.'

I pressed the middle. My badge doesn't play 'Jingle Bells', but Santa still lights up, and he goes *Ho, ho, ho* instead.

'I love it,' I said, and kissed him on the cheek.

There was an enormous Christmas tree standing in the hall when I got home, and Flora, Twig and Jas were all sitting on the stairs as Zach and Dad struggled to get it straight. Zach is basically at our house all the time now. I think he's been here every single day after school. Twig has got him working on the tree house and Jas keeps dragging him off for secret talks (which really annoys Flora), and Mum has asked him to stay for supper twice. She's even invited him to come for Christmas.

I don't care what Dodi says about boys needing time and space. I just sent Jake a picture of all of us including Zach decorating the tree. 'Wish you were here too!' I wrote, because it was true. Then I told him I was wearing his badge and added lots of kisses.

Saturday 21 December

Dodi is going skiing with her parents for Christmas this year, but before she left we spent the whole morning at Portobello Market rummaging through second-hand-book stalls until I found exactly what I wanted for Jake, two almost perfect early 1980s *X-Men* comics.

'Nice,' Zach said when I showed them to him. 'How much d'you pay?'

I told him. Then when he looked shocked I said I could have paid a load more, but the person who sold them to me gave me a good price because one of them is a bit torn. Zach, who is kind, said they were a really cool present and Jake would be thrilled.

Flora, who is not kind, told me later that Zach said I'd been completely cheated. She said 1980s comics weren't valuable at all, and next time I should ask Zach for his advice, because he knew all about it.

'I can't believe Jake buys you a singing badge and you spend all that money on *X-Men* comics,' Flora said.

'It's not about the money,' I said, and then I texted Jake to tell him I've got him the best present ever.

He wrote, 'You shouldn't have, I only got you that badge.'

I wrote, 'I love that badge,' and he sent me a smiley face.

It made me feel all warm inside.

Wednesday 25 December

It has been a good Christmas.

Yesterday was Iris's death day. We went to church again, all six of us, not to a service or anything, just us, like the other day with Mum.

'Everything is changing,' I told Iris in church yesterday. 'Mum and Dad are having a baby, Twig and Jas are growing up, Flora has this boyfriend who is practically living with us, and I'm going out with Jake. Remember Jake, from primary school? I like him a lot. Flora loves change, but I don't, not really. I was just getting used to the way things were, you know? I don't know if I'm ready for a whole new set of things.'

Dad was praying next to me, his lips moving and everything, and since I know he doesn't believe in God, I knew that he was talking to Iris too. He saw me looking at him and held out his hand.

'Do you think she minds about the baby?' he asked.

'I think she's sad she won't be here for it, but I don't think she minds,' I told him.

Dad blinked very fast so I wouldn't notice he was crying.

'Don't be scared,' I whispered.

'I'm not scared,' he whispered back.

'Me neither.' I smiled, and he smiled back.

'I'm ****** petrified,' he admitted.

Zach didn't come for Christmas Day, despite Mum's invitation. He really wanted to, but Zoran says that family is family, and took him to visit his grandfather in hospital in the country, and they're stopping at the Richmond Hill Retirement Home on the way back to visit Zoran's great-aunt Alina.

Flora says Zach was really hoping his mum would come for Christmas, but he still hasn't heard from her. We are going to Zoran's for lunch tomorrow, but yesterday and today were just about us. It was a completely uneventful day. Just the six of us, shuffling about in our pyjamas, opening presents and eating cake for breakfast and going for a walk because Mum said we had to. Flora cooked dinner. She says she needs the practice for when she leaves home to go and live in a flat with lots of other actors, probably in New York or Los Angeles or somewhere. This basically meant that all of us except Mum (who was resting) and Dad (who was writing – apparently holidays don't count if you are a creative genius) spent most of the afternoon in the kitchen, which ended up looking even worse than when Mum cooks. After all our hard work, the turkey was tough, the vegetables weren't properly cooked and the potatoes were completely burned because Flora decided to do a one-woman rendition of *A Christmas Carol* when she was meant to be lightly parboiling them. But Jas decorated the table with Christmas-themed Haribos, Twig made rum-and-raisin reindeer-shaped cookies, I made gravy out of a packet which made everything taste nice, if not delicious, and Dad drank too much port as usual and fell asleep on the sofa with Mum while we were clearing up.

'Look!' Jas dragged us over to look at them. Mum lay at one end of the sofa with her head thrown back and her mouth open, snoring lightly, both hands on her tummy. Dad lay at the other end, his head turned into the cushions, snoring much more loudly, completely unaware of Ron and Hermione, also sleeping and snoring, stretched out across his lap.

Absolutely nothing happened this Christmas, but Mum got what she wanted: it was one of the best ones since Iris died.

The Film Diaries of
Bluebell Gadsby

Scene Six (Transcript)
Boxing Day Lunch

INTERIOR. DAY.

Inside Zoran's flat. The small table
by the window is crowded round with
chairs and the remains of lunch
(casserole of pork with apricots,
shredded greens with chestnuts, cheese
and herb dumplings, trifle). ZORAN,
JAS and TWIG sit cross-legged on the
floor in front of the coffee table,
eating traditional Bosnian biscuits
known as bear paws, made with walnuts
and tossed in sugar (a present from
Alina). MOTHER and ZACH sit on the
sofa, watching FLORA, who stands
before them, trying to act out *Pirates
of the Caribbean: Dead Man's Chest*,
while CAMERAMAN (Blue) films.

They are playing charades.

Jas, Twig and Cameraman knew the title the moment Flora started to act it out, but Mother and Zach haven't got a clue.

MOTHER
Harry Potter!

ZACH
Batman!

MOTHER
Dracula! Robin Hood! Les Misérables!

The doorbell rings. Zoran pads over to the intercom to buzz open the door to the street, then flings open the door to the flat and stands straight like a soldier, holding out the biscuit tin. Nobody else pays attention. They are expecting Father, who skipped lunch to work on his book.

ZACH
Pirates of the Caribbean!

Flora squeals and jumps up and down, making wild hand gestures.

                    ZACH
        Curse of the Black Pearl! *At World's
        End*!! *On Stranger Tides*!!!

                    FLORA
        YOU ARE BOTH COMPLETELY USELESS!

                    MOTHER
        I know, I know! *Dead Man's
        Chest*!!!!!

                    FLORA
        FINALLY!

By now, Mother and Zach are crying with laughter and hugging each other. Flora drops down next to them, telling them again they were useless. Mother hugs her too.
    Zoran comes in from the hallway. Alone.

                    ZORAN
              (very serious)
        Zach, you have a visitor.

Zach looks up, still laughing, from the sofa where Twig and Jas have joined them. A woman walks into the room behind Zoran. Tall, pale, with purple smudges under her dark eyes and long black hair, wrapped in a pale grey cashmere coat which she hugs to her body as if, despite the mild weather, she is cold. She looks like a fairy-tale queen, or maybe a witch. She also looks familiar.

Mother, Flora, Jas and Twig, sensing something is wrong, move away from Zach, who scrambles up from the sofa to stand before the stranger.

ZACH
Mum!

Mother signals to Cameraman to stop filming.

Picture goes black.

Zach stared like he couldn't believe his eyes.

'Surprise!' she said, but she sounded nervous.

Zach opened his mouth, but no sound came out. Her face fell. He took a step towards her and held out his hand, but it was shaking. He let it drop like he didn't know what to do with it.

Mum pushed herself up and came to stand beside him, putting her own hand out to steady his.

'We're very pleased to meet you,' she said. 'We're all so fond of Zach.'

Zach's mother looked round the room, took in Jas and Twig on the sofa, Zoran, Flora, me, before coming back to let her eyes rest on Zach.

'Won't you sit down?'

Zoran gestured towards the sofa. Twig and Jas jumped off it. Flora also came to stand beside Zach and took his other hand. His mother sat down, still wearing her coat.

'Say something, Zach,' Flora whispered, but he still couldn't speak.

'This was a mistake.' Zach's mother was already back on her feet. 'I have to go,' she said, and hurried out of the room. Zach came back to life, shouted

'Mum!' and ran after her. After a moment's hesitation, Zoran followed.

'No,' Mum said, as Flora started to go after Zoran, and then she cried, 'Twig, stop that, it's dangerous!' because he was leaning right out of the window, looking into the street.

'You can see really well from here,' he said, and we all leaned out, ignoring Mum. Down on the pavement, Zach's mother was trying to get into a car but Zach stood in her way. She pushed him, jumped into the car and drove away.

Even four storeys up, we heard Zach shout. 'Mum!'

He ran after her but she didn't stop. He went halfway down the street and then gave up.

Flora ran downstairs, but Zoran got there. He pulled Zach out of the road and then he just stood there, with his arms around him, holding him and holding him while Zach cried like I've never seen a boy cry in my entire life.

Friday 27 December

Flora says she was right all along and that Zach's mother is a witch. She went to see Zach this morning, and came into my room when she got back to tell me about it. I knew the minute she came in that she was in a really bad mood.

'I don't care how nice she ever was to him,' she said. 'All that going to the seaside and tea at the Ritz. She's horrible and I hate her.'

'What happened?'

She flopped down on my bed and closed her eyes. 'We quarrelled,' she sighed.

This is how it happened. When Flora arrived at Zoran's flat, he said that Zach had gone to the park with his basketball, so she followed him there.

'He was all alone on the court,' she said. 'Just like the first time I spoke to him.'

She watched him play until he stopped, and then she called out to him. Normally, she says, his whole face lights up when he sees her, but today he just said, 'Oh it's you,' and that's when they had their first argument, right there on the basketball court. Flora said, 'Aren't you going to kiss me hello?' and Zach said, 'What's the point?' and Flora wasn't quite sure what to answer to that so she said, 'I'm so sorry about your mum,' and Zach said, 'Yeah, well,' and they sat down on a bench, and Flora said, 'I can't believe she could be so horrible.' Zach said, 'It's not like that,' and Flora said, 'Well what is it like then?'

and suddenly they were shouting at each other, all about Zach's mum and how Flora with her ******* perfect family could never understand what it was like for him.

'I said don't talk about my family like that, and then we yelled some more, and he left.'

'He really said that about us?' I asked.

Flora said yes, he did.

'But we're not perfect,' I said. 'We're so very far from perfect.'

'That's not all,' Flora said. She was huddled up in a ball on my bed, with a blanket wrapped around her, and for the first time I realised that she looked scared as well as angry. 'I think she was there, Blue,' she said.

'What do you mean?'

'Zach's mother. He stormed off and didn't see her, but I did. Standing at the edge of the court, you know where the big trees are? She must have been hiding there the whole time.'

'Are you sure it was her?'

'I didn't see her face,' Flora admitted. 'And she was wearing a hat, but it was the same coat, and she *was* watching us. It was creepy, Blue.'

'We should tell the parents,' I said.

'Tell them what?' Flora asked. 'They'll only go

and talk to Zoran, and then Zach will be even more furious with me.' And then she repeated how much she hated Zach's stupid mother, and stormed off to talk to Tamsin.

Zoran spoke to Mr Rudowski yesterday to tell him what had happened, and also to ask him to explain Zach's mother's behaviour, but Mr Rudowski was so upset that one of the nurses took the telephone away from him and told Zoran to let him be. I overheard Zoran tell Mum when he came round this evening to bring back a bag she forgot at his flat. He's spoken to Alina about it too. Alina says she doesn't know any details, but that Wanda (Zach's mother) had always been what she calls *problematic* and had a *history of mental illness*.

Zoran is taking Zach away. Alina has a friend with a little cottage by the sea near Brighton, and he has agreed to lend it to Zoran. 'It will do us both good to get away for a while,' Zoran said.

Flora says good riddance and she never wants to see Zach again, but I know she doesn't mean it. She keeps checking her phone for messages from him. And Jas is upset as well. She just came into my room too, as I was writing this, and asked did I know when Zach was coming back.

I said that I had no idea and she crept out again, looking dejected.

Saturday 28 December

Grandma has arrived, on her way back to Devon from Arizona. Dad went to fetch her at the airport, and she is going to stay for a week, while Dad whisks Mum away to Paris for a few days of Being Romantic.

Having Grandma here has cheered everybody up. Grandma can be maddening and she is even more bossy than Flora, but it's difficult to be miserable when she's around. For one thing, she is one of the loudest people I know. She landed at six o'clock this morning. By half past seven she was in our kitchen cooking the most enormous fry-up I have ever seen, as well as a skyscraper of pancakes.

'AMERICAN BREAKFASTS!' Grandma bellowed, pouring maple syrup over everything. 'ABSOLUTELY MARVELLOUS! NO NEED TO EAT ANYTHING ELSE FOR THE REST OF THE DAY!'

Grandma has her own view about the baby. 'AT

YOUR AGE?' she cried when they told her. 'ARE YOU MAD?'

'I'm only forty-two,' Mum said, and Grandma sniffed and said forty-two should be old enough to see sense but she supposed there was no stopping some people. I could see Mum really wanted to storm out of the kitchen but also that she was torn because everything tastes so delicious when it is covered in maple syrup.

'How are you all taking the news?' Grandma asked more quietly when I went up to her room to watch her unpack.

'It was a bit of a shock at first.' I thought it was probably best not to mention Iris, or Dad being scared. Grandma can be very understanding and she is one of my favourite people in the whole world, but it's not always easy to talk to her when she's being disapproving. 'We're really happy now,' I said. 'Dad keeps telling Mum's tummy that he loves it. Twig is convinced he's going to get a brother, and Flora wants to play at being a mum with her boyfriend Zach, or at least she did until they had a fight.'

Then I got distracted, because Grandma had pulled a very torn and battered copy of *Jane Eyre* from her case, and I remembered that I'm supposed to read the first three chapters over the holidays but with all the baby excitement and then Zach I had completely forgotten, and not for the first time I thought that there was something a little bit magic about Grandma, who is able to produce exactly what you need, when you need it.

'Ah, the boyfriend,' Grandma said. 'Your father told me all about him. And what about you? Are you in love yet?'

There's never any use lying to her.

'I'm not sure about being in love,' I told her. 'But I am going out with my friend Jake.'

Grandma said, 'Well I hope you've got him on a good short rein.'

I said I didn't really know what that meant, and Grandma said it meant she hoped that Jake was being nice to me, and also that I wasn't letting him walk all over me if he wasn't. 'I know what you're like, young Bluebell,' she said. 'You're too forgiving.'

I fingered my Santa badge. 'He's very nice to me,' I said.

Grandma gave me one of her sharp looks.

'Really,' I insisted. 'He is.'

I didn't want to tell her I haven't heard from Jake since he sent me that smiley way before Christmas. For a start I didn't think she'd approve, but also perhaps this is normal. Just because Flora and Zach are permanently joined at the hip (or used to be, anyway) doesn't mean everybody has to be like that. And anyway, how much can you say in a text?

Grandma was still looking at me.

'Some things fit and some just don't,' she said. 'Not enough people remember that.' And then she changed the subject and said why didn't I read *Jane Eyre* out loud to her while she finished unpacking.

I've been reading it all day. 'It's a lot better than I thought it would be,' I told her this evening at supper, and she smiled and said wasn't it wonderful when life turned out that way.

Sunday 29 December

Flora is starting to get twitchy about New Year's Eve, and the fact that she still hasn't heard from Zach. She was going to go down to Trafalgar Square with him to see the fireworks, and now she doesn't know what to do.

'Can't you go with Tamsin instead?' I asked, and she said that wasn't the point. She called Zoran to ask him when they were coming back and he said he didn't know. Then she asked him why Zach wasn't answering her texts, and he said he didn't know about that either, but to give him time.

'How much time does he need?' Flora moaned after she'd spoken to Zoran. 'I've said I'm sorry about a million times, even though he hasn't once apologised to me. Just because he's so worked up about his crazy mother, why does that mean he can't talk to me?'

Grandma said boys often find it difficult to think about more than one thing at once.

'He'd better come back soon,' said Twig. 'Or we'll never finish the tree house.'

'I really, really need to speak to him,' whispered Jas. 'Can I have his phone number?'

Flora shouted, 'For God's sake, no wonder he doesn't want to see me any more!' and you could tell she was going to cry because her nose was blotchy. 'The way you go on,' she screamed, 'you've probably scared him off!' And then she ran upstairs, and sure enough she hadn't even reached the landing before she burst into noisy sobs.

That was this morning. Then Dodi rang, to say she was back and what was *I* doing for New Year's.

'Are you seeing Jake?' she asked. 'Shall we all do something together?'

I said Jake was still at his gran's, and Dodi said,

'No, he's back.' And then her voice went a bit funny and she said, 'Didn't you know that?' and even though we were on the phone I blushed, and said no I didn't but it didn't matter.

'He's been back since Boxing Day,' Dodi said. 'I spoke to Colin last night. I can't believe he hasn't called you.'

'We're not really like that,' I said, but I couldn't really believe it either.

'You're his *girlfriend*,' Dodi said. 'What you need to do is call him up *right now* to tell him he can't treat you like that. On second thoughts, don't do that, it makes you sound a bit desperate. *I'll* call him.'

I held the phone away from my ear and looked at it. Dodi carried on talking. I don't think she even noticed I wasn't listening.

'I never even wanted to go out with Jake in the first place,' I told her.

'Well why did you then?' she asked.

'Because you told me to. You're always telling me what to do.'

'Only because you can never decide anything for yourself.'

I hung up on her. She called straight back, but I ignored her.

It seems quite astonishing to me that Flora and I both have boyfriends who are ignoring us, but at least Zach has the excuse of his mad mother. Jake's just being rude.

I read a load more of *Jane Eyre* today, and what I think is this: if Jane Eyre, who was a weed, could stand up to Mr Rochester, who was rich and powerful, at a time when women were supposed to be meek and never complain, then I can stand up to Jake and ask him what is going on.

The Saga of Bluebell and Jake

Heartbreaks and Milkshakes

EXTERIOR. DAY, ABOUT THREE O'CLOCK IN THE AFTERNOON.

BLUE, carefully attired in black skinny jeans (her own), a silvery sequin jumper (borrowed from Dodi long ago and worn under her orders), duffle coat, her Santa badge and one of Flora's hats, shelters at a bus stop in front of Jake's house, waiting for him to come out.

The front door opens. JAKE emerges. Blue breaks into a discreet run and catches up with him.

                    BLUE
        (masterful, though inwardly quaking)
            Let's go for a coffee?

                    JAKE
              (looking terrified)
                     Er.

                    BLUE
       (still displaying a strength she
                does not feel)
       Excellent. Let's go to Home Sweet
                    Home.

Cut to interior, Home Sweet Home.
Blue and Jake sit at a table by
the window. She (being sophisticated)
has a cappuccino. He has ordered a
chocolate milkshake.

                    BLUE
        (presenting a gift-wrapped package)
       This is your Christmas present. It
       took me ages to find it. I hope you
                   like it.

                    JAKE
        (not looking at her, mumbling so
                hard he is virtually
                incomprehensible)
       I can't go out with you any more.

                     139

BLUE
(ploughing on)
I bought it because I know you love
the *X-Men* films and it reminded me of
when we went to the cinema. You know,
with Colin and Tom.

JAKE
(as above)
When I was in Australia at my
auntie's wedding I met my cousin's
best friend Tallulah and fell in love
with her. I felt really bad because
of you, and so I tried to forget
about her and make it work with you,
but then I found out she was coming
over for the holidays. They were the
Australian friends who came to stay
with us before Christmas. After us,
they went to stay with Gran. That's
why I left London early, to go and
see her. She has gone back to
Australia now, but I still love her
and I don't want to lie to you any
more. I'm sorry.

                    BLUE
                 (shakily)
    I can't believe you didn't tell me
                  before.

                    JAKE
                  (etc.)
    I didn't mean it to happen. As soon
    as we arrived in Melbourne we drove
    out to the beach to look at the
    penguins and Tallulah was there. Ever
    since I've been very confused.

                    BLUE
             I love penguins.

                    JAKE
             So does Tallulah.

                    BLUE
    I suppose I'd better go then.
                (hesitates)
    You can keep the present.

She rises slowly and walks away
feeling crushed and humiliated. At the
door, she turns one last time with

tears in her eyes. Jake is already talking on his phone. Blue, feeling like she is in a real movie, strides back across the cafe to the table where Jake sits.

BLUE
Are you talking to her?

JAKE
What? No! Of course not, it's nighttime in Australia!

Blue carefully takes back the comics. She removes the badge and puts it down where the comics were. And *then* she picks up Jake's milkshake and empties it over his head.

I forgot I was cross with Dodi. The first thing I did when I left the cafe was call her to tell her what I'd done.

'His milkshake?' Dodi repeated. 'All over his head? Oh, I'm so proud of you!'

I've never heard her laugh so hard at anything.

I think it's the most outrageous thing I have ever done in my entire life. In fact, I think it may be the *only* outrageous thing I've ever done, and it felt fantastic. I ran almost the whole way home. It was raining really hard and I didn't have an umbrella, but I didn't care. It could have been hailing golf balls and I wouldn't have noticed.

My mood changed as I got wetter and colder. I passed the cemetery where Jas found the kittens, and went in. I found Violet Buttercream's grave and Jas was right, it is a nice place to sit. 'I should be crying,' I told myself. The rain fell harder and the light grew dimmer. I was freezing by now. I thought really hard about how my heart had been broken into a thousand tiny pieces, but still the tears didn't come, because what I mainly felt was angry.

All that time wasted thinking about Jake when he

wasn't ever thinking about me. He used to be my *friend*. He should never have lied to me.

Jas was sitting at the kitchen table doing homework when I got in. I put the kettle on for tea then sank on to the sofa and sighed.

In the proper film of my life, this would be the moment when they play soulful music with a close-up of me gazing moodily out of the window looking brave. The moment when everything is about to change. An *important* moment.

Jas didn't even look up from her books.

'Jake and I have split up,' I told her.

Jas sighed, gathered up her papers and stomped upstairs.

I followed her. On the landing outside our bedrooms, Grandma was lecturing Twig on the rules of football indoors.

'The ball should *not* be muddy,' Grandma scolded.

'But I *like* mud,' Twig replied.

'I've split up with Jake,' I said, but neither of them replied because at that moment Flora stole the limelight as usual, and started screaming on the phone downstairs.

'I don't care about my A levels!' Flora shouted. 'I

want to be an actress and get as far away from my life as possible!'

We all crept down to see what was going on. She was standing in the hall, dripping water everywhere because she doesn't have an umbrella either, yelling at Mum on her phone because she just learned that she got the part she auditioned for weeks ago but Mum won't let her do it because the play opens right in the middle of Flora's exams.

'WELL I DON'T EXACTLY APPROVE OF YOU HAVING A BABY!' Flora was yelling, which was when Grandma took her phone.

'I'LL TAKE CARE OF THIS END, CASSIE!' Grandma shouts even louder than normal when she's on the phone. 'THE MOST IMPORTANT THING RIGHT NOW IS FOR YOU TO STAY CALM!'

After she had hung up, Grandma gave us all a lecture. With Mum in the state she's in, Grandma says, we must be model children. 'That means NO SHOUTING,' she said. 'No mud, no stomping, no moping over boyfriends.'

'Actually,' I said, 'I am not moping over him. If anyone ever listened to me ...'

'And no interrupting,' said Grandma, and told us all to go away while she gave some serious thought to what she was going to do with us because it was obvious we all needed a distraction.

I went down to find her in her room when the others had all gone to bed, and told her about Jake and the milkshake. Her reaction was almost exactly the same as Dodi's. She said it was the funniest thing she'd ever heard and she had never been more proud of me. Then she said that Jake was a snake, a rat and a scoundrel, and asked me if I was very upset.

I thought about my answer very carefully. 'I *am* upset,' I said. 'But not as much as I think I should be. Mainly I just feel really, really stupid.'

Grandma said Jake was the one who was stupid, preferring anyone to her granddaughter, and then she started to chuckle and said, oh to have been a fly on the wall at the Home Sweet Home when I threw the milkshake. I just heard her go into the bathroom, and she was still laughing.

Going out with someone because you feel a bit sorry for them is a *really bad idea*. Next year is going to be different, I've decided. Next year I am only going to do things I actually want to do.

WHOLESOME EXERCISE is what Grandma has decided to do with us, and so today she marched us all over to Jas's stables for a riding lesson.

We found Gloria huddled over a gas fire in the tack room going through a wad of papers with a calculator on her knee.

'Bills,' Flora whispered. 'Red ones.'

Gloria sighed when she saw us and explained that if we were good enough she would take us for a ride on the common, but that for our first day we had to pass a test to make sure it was safe and the first thing we should do was tack up the horses. She showed us which ponies we were riding and then the phone rang and she marched back to the tack room and left us with water dripping down our necks, because obviously it was still raining, clutching saddles and reins and wondering which bits went where.

'You heard her,' Grandma said. 'Get on with it.'

'I have no idea what to do,' Twig said.

'You are here to learn,' Grandma said.

'I know what to do,' Jas said.

'This is a terrible place,' Flora announced.

'It's a community project,' Grandma corrected her. 'It was set up to help children in need.'

'Are we children in need?' asked Twig.

'I am,' Flora grumbled under her breath. 'In need of dry clothes, a boyfriend who calls me back and a grandmother who isn't insane.'

As far as the riding went, we were all hopeless except Jas. The only lessons we have ever had before were with Grandma and boiled down to GO FASTER AND DON'T FALL OFF, but Gloria has a different approach. She made us practise all sorts of exercises like figures of eight and changing reins and other stuff none of us understood, first walking, then trotting, until our legs ached and our brains were completely confused.

'I thought that was quite fascinating,' Grandma said when the lesson was over.

'I'm afraid I can't come back,' Flora told Gloria firmly. 'I'm doing my A levels in the summer and I have to study really, really hard.'

Twig, who fell off more times than anybody else, said that now he was playing on a team he really had to focus on his football. I wanted to say I couldn't come either, because I have decided that I really, *really* don't like horses, but I didn't want to disappoint Grandma, and also I remembered the calculator and the papers and the way Gloria sighed when we arrived. So instead I said I would love to come back next weekend with Jas and join her regular lesson.

Flora checked her phone again on the way home, but there were still no messages from Zach.

'Do you think he's had an accident?' Jas asked.

'Maybe he fell under a train.' Twig was on my laptop looking at train timetables online. I know for a fact he finds trains really, really boring, but Maisie has asked him to babysit her little brother again on Monday after school, and Twig is determined to impress the kid with his extensive knowledge. Dodi, who is fascinated by Twig's love life, says surely he must realise how Maisie is using him, but Twig swears she's not like that.

'Maybe he was standing on a railway bridge,' Twig said now, 'and it was raining, and he leaned over a bit too much and slipped under the 4.23 from Paddington.'

'Could that happen?' Jas looked horrified.

'I think it's quite unlikely,' I said. 'And I'm sure Zoran would have told us.'

'CAN YOU PLEASE ALL STOP TALKING ABOUT MY BOYFRIEND LIKE HE'S DEAD?' Flora yelled.

'Loads of people fall under trains,' Twig said.

Jas said Twig's new hobby was horrible and that

Maisie Carter wasn't even pretty. Twig said she was. Jas said she wasn't. Twig said anyway it was none of her business. Jas said he was making it her business by being so annoying. Flora said that if they didn't shut up she'd push them both under the nearest train.

Wednesday 1 January: New Year's Day

It's half past midnight, and it's a brand new year.

Flora did go out with Tamsin in the end. They went into town to see the fireworks. Dodi's staying over. She said Colin had invited her to his parents' annual New Year's Eve party, but she didn't go because she knew Jake was going to be there. Grandma ordered a Chinese takeaway and baked a three-layered red velvet cake with cream cheese, vanilla and ginger icing, and we ate the whole thing in front of the TV watching the countdown, while Jas tried to teach the kittens to ride my old skateboard. The list of things Jas is trying to teach the kittens is growing longer by the day. So far, they have failed to learn to come when they are called, to only do their business in the litter tray, not to climb up curtains and to sit on command.

'They're a lot less trainable than the rats,' Jas complained. 'I could get them to do almost anything.'

Personally, I thought skateboarding was overly ambitious, but Twig found a sort of solution by putting Hermione on the board when she was asleep and launching her across the room before she could wake up. It didn't last very long, because she was awake within about half a second and flew from the skateboard to beneath the sofa so fast she was almost just a blur, but it *was* funny. Jas said that it wasn't proper training at all, but even she laughed.

Friday 3 January

Mum and Dad came home last night. Dad took Grandma to the station early this morning, but her leaving has been completely overshadowed by what has happened to Flora.

Mum and Flora both went back to bed after Grandma left, so only Twig, Jas and I were up when the post arrived with a letter for Flora. It came in a bright green envelope which was posted in Glasgow and we all had a good look at it because it's quite rare for any of us to get actual mail. Then when

Flora finally got up, we crowded on to the landing to watch as she picked it up from the table in the hall.

'Perhaps it's from Zach,' whispered Jas.

'It's from *Scotland*,' said Twig.

'Shh!' I said. Down beneath us, Flora had opened the envelope and was standing stock still, reading. When she finished, she leaned against the wall, staring into nothing. Then she read it again.

'Do you think it *is* from Zach?' Jas insisted.

'Do you really think Zach would send a letter in a bright green envelope?' I asked.

'Perhaps it's all he could find,' she said. 'Perhaps it's his favourite colour.'

'Mum! *Mum!* MUM!' Flora yelled.

'She's still sleeping,' I called down as softly as I could.

Flora tore past me into Mum's room. 'Read this!' she shouted and shoved the letter under Mum's nose.

Mum moaned, 'Flora, I am *asleep*.'

'Then listen!' Flora brandished the letter, which was also bright green, waving it about until she had our full attention, and then she began to read.

Dear Miss Gadsby,

We were most impressed by your recent audition. It was a very ambitious role, and we

felt that you would have tackled it well. What a
shame the production coincides with your A-level
timetable, though of course it goes without saying
that your exams must come first . . .

'I did tell you,' Mum murmured, but Flora ignored
her.

You may know that three years ago I set up a new
training facility for young actors such as yourself.
Foundation courses run from September to June,
and I am writing now to offer you a place for next
year. These places are very limited, so please let
me know as soon as possible if you are interested.
You will find all the relevant information
concerning dates, accommodation and fees in the
accompanying information leaflet.
    Yours sincerely,
    Thomasina Foulkes Watson

Flora was shouting louder than Grandma by the end
of the letter.

'Who', Mum croaked, 'is Thomasina
Foulkes-Watson?'

'Thomasina Foulkes-Watson', Flora announced,
'is probably the most influential talent scout, casting

consultant and producer of new plays in Britain. Her school is amazing. You have to be invited to go, and all the best actors teach there. It's like being given a place at . . . Oxford or Cambridge or Harvard or something.'

'But you're going to King's.' Mum was completely awake now. 'They offered you a place and you're starting in October and you're going to read English and Drama.'

Flora stared back down at her letter before replying. She folded it very carefully and put it back in its envelope, and then she said, very softly, 'No, I'm not.'

She and Mum looked at each other for ages.

'No,' Mum said at last. She put both her hands on her tummy, like she was asking the baby what it thought of all this, then she held one out to Flora. 'No,' she repeated. 'I can see you're not.'

I crept down to the kitchen with Twig and Jas. Twig hasn't baked anything for a while, but I found a packet of chocolate biscuits in the cupboard. We squeezed up on the sofa to eat them.

'It's all very exciting,' I said.

'She's going to live in Scotland?' asked Jas.

'I can't imagine this house without Flora,' said Twig, and we were all silent for a while, trying to picture it and failing.

I just went out because as I was writing I thought I heard crying from Flora's room, and I was right. She was lying in bed, fully dressed, with the duvet over her head and her face pressed into the pillow. I thought about stroking her hair, but you can never be too sure how Flora is going to react to things like that, so I just sat down next to her instead.

'Why aren't you happy?' I asked.

'I am!' she sniffed.

'You sound it,' I said. She poked her head out from under the covers. Her face was all puffy, with little salt tracks from her tears and mascara halfway down her cheeks.

'You look it too,' I said. Flora sniffed even louder.

'Of course I'm happy,' she said, and then her lip started to wobble again and these big fat tears began to splash down her face. I had to lean really close to work out what she was saying.

'It's Zach,' she wailed finally between sobs. 'If I go away to Scotland, it means we're definitely over.'

'Not necessarily,' I said. I didn't think it was the right time to talk to her about the fickleness of men, especially given Zach's current uncommunicative behaviour. 'There are loads of very successful long-distance relationships,' I told her.

'Name one,' Flora wailed. I said well, look at all

those men who went off to the First World War and spent four years in trenches with their wives waiting faithfully for them at home. Flora said that didn't exactly make her feel better since most of them *died*, and what was she going to do if he did fall under a train and did I think that was possible?

'It's possible,' I said. 'But like I said the other day, I think it's very unlikely.'

'Don't go,' she sniffed. She wriggled to the edge of her bed and I lay down next to her.

'Boys are rubbish,' I whispered.

'I know,' she whispered back. 'But I do love him so much. Is it true you threw a milkshake over Jake?'

'How do you know about that?'

'Tamsin's mum told us. She heard it from a friend of Jake's mum. I should have said something sooner, but you know . . .' She gave me a watery smile. 'Way to go, little sister,' she said. And then she started crying again.

I stayed there for ages, long after Flora stopped crying and went to sleep. I thought Dodi would probably have told everyone, but I can't believe it's got as far as Tamsin's mum. There are just two days left till school starts again. Basically, someone has to do something massively dramatic, or the whole world is going to be talking about me.

Flora flipped over in her sleep and nearly hit me in the face. I slipped out from under her duvet and pulled it up around her shoulders. I wish there was something I could do for her, but I don't think an accidental meeting in the park would work a second time.

I have found out why Zach means so much to Jas. She told me everything when we went back to the stables this afternoon and were brushing our horses down afterwards. Their stalls are side by side, with wooden bars you can talk through, and Jas said could she ask me a question. Then she asked did I think Zach and Flora had split up, and if so, did that mean we would never see Zach again?

I said I didn't know.

'Do you think they will?'

I said maybe, when she goes to Scotland. I'd like to think mere distance wouldn't come between them, but look at me and Jake. I mean, I know Australia is a lot further than Scotland, but he was gone less than a month and he fell in love with Tallulah *on the second day*. And then I heard Jas sniff and I asked, 'Are you crying?' and she said no, she was perfectly fine, just a bit allergic to horses.

'That's ridiculous,' I said, and then she started to cry properly.

'I tried to call him!' she sniffed. 'I got his number from Flora's phone, but he didn't answer, and I left a message but he hasn't called back, and I *need* him!'

I really thought I knew what was wrong with her then. I wanted to say to her, it's perfectly natural to have a crush on your older sister's boyfriend, trust me it happens all the time, except I wasn't sure if she knew about me liking Flora's old boyfriend Joss last year, and if she didn't I would rather it stayed that way.

'He's the only one who ever LISTENS to me,' Jas cried through her tears. And that was when she told me everything, and it is nothing I would have guessed in a million years.

Jas is a poet.

And Zach is the only person who has ever read her poems.

'He really liked them,' she said. 'He said I had "definite talent". He was going to . . .'

'Going to what?' I asked.

'There's this competition,' Jas said. 'I read about it in the newspaper. He was helping me with it, and now I've got to the actual final, and I have to *perform* it, stand up and recite it and everything, and I DON'T KNOW WHAT TO DO!'

I stared at her in astonishment. 'That's wonderful, Jas,' I told her.

'But what am I going to do?' she cried.

'About what?'

'I asked you for help before but you weren't interested,' Jas said. 'Nobody is *ever* interested. It's all *oh my boyfriend my acting career my hair gel my documentary my baby*. It's never, EVER about me. Zach is the only one who cared and even he must have been pretending because now he's GONE!'

'Do you mind about the baby?' I asked.

'Of course not!' she said. 'Do you?'

'Of course not,' I said.

'I'm just sick of being the youngest,' said Jas. 'It used to be fun, but then you get left behind. At least once the baby's born people might stop treating me like a little kid and leave me alone.'

Jas is clearly as confused about the baby as I am.

'When we get home,' I said, 'let's tell the parents about the competition. Dad's a writer. Maybe he can help.'

'If you tell Mum and Dad I write poetry,' Jas said, 'I swear I will never, ever speak to you again.'

My pony was growing restless. I'd stopped brushing her to talk to Jas, and I think she was wondering what I was still doing in her box. She nudged me with her head like she was pushing me towards the door.

'I don't understand why you need Zach,' I said. 'I mean, I can understand you're sad he's not around to hear about it and everything, but you're in the final now. I bet you'll even win.'

'I can't win.'

'You might.'

'I CAN'T!!!' Jas shouted, and then she started talking really, really slowly, like I was really, really stupid. 'This is not a children's competition. It is the West London Poetic Society's Annual Open to All Competition, but it is *not* "open to all" because it is for people aged sixteen years and over. I can't win, BECAUSE I AM NINE YEARS OLD. It is *spectacularly* unfair.'

'But why do you need Zach?' I asked.

'I need Zach,' Jas said, 'to pretend to be me.'

Flopsy gave up on nudging, and nipped me on the shoulder. It hurt. I yelled. Flopsy pushed me out of the box.

Bill was sitting on a bench right outside the door,

polishing a bridle. 'You want to be more careful around horses,' he said.

'Were you *listening*?' I cried, and he shrugged and said, 'Sounds like someone needs to have a word with this lad.' He looked straight at me when he said that.

'Me?' I asked.

'Someone's got to,' he said.

'He's not answering his phone,' I told him.

'More than one way of talking to a person,' he said.

Sunday 5 January

I spent ages writing to Zach.

I wrote loads about understanding how strange it must have been to see his mum again after so long, and how hurtful her leaving must have been.

I wrote about Iris and how I know what it feels like to miss someone you really love.

I wrote about how annoying Flora can be, and how when they quarrelled she was probably a load more hurtful than she told me.

Then I got annoyed, because even though this is Zach and not Jake, I am still wasting my time worrying about finding the right thing to say to a boy, and I limited my letter to facts.

'I'm truly sorry about your mum,' I wrote. 'But the point is, we are here, and she is not. We miss you, and we are not going away.'

Then I wrote about Flora and how much she missed him and how she hadn't stopped moping since he went away, and about Jas, and how upset *she* was because of her competition. I finished by telling him that if he wanted to finish with Flora, he should be brave enough to do it properly, and otherwise he should come round and see her immediately.

'PS,' I added. 'Flora *is* upset, but she may choose to play it cool. I recommend flowers and chocolate.'

I wrote the letter very late last night and got up early this morning to cycle over to Zoran's flat before anyone was awake to ask me what I was doing. With school starting tomorrow, I assumed they would be back soon, if they weren't back already. After I'd put it through the letterbox I sat and stared at the letterbox for a while, wondering if I'd done the right thing, and then I decided there was nothing I could do about it anyway, so I came home.

At lunchtime Mum got a phone call from Zoran, saying they were back in London.

At half past two Flora announced that she was going to bed with a fever and that she might never get up again.

At five minutes past four the doorbell rang, and it was Zach, clutching a bunch of tulips. Twig answered the door, which was good, because anyone else would have made a fuss. All Twig did was say, 'Oh, cool, you're back,' and yell upstairs for Flora.

Flora didn't play it cool.

She appeared at the top of the stairs much too quickly for someone dying of a fever. Zach held up the flowers. Until today I never truly understood what people meant when they said 'she flew down the stairs'. One second Flora was on the landing, the next she was in the hall with her arms around Zach's neck. Her feet didn't touch a single step.

'You don't hate me!' she cried.

'I brought chocolate too,' Zach said, and then they didn't speak for a while because they were too busy kissing. Then Jas appeared, and Zach was all 'Hey, Jas' and she said, 'You're back!' Zach said, 'Yeah, and we've got work to do,' and Jas beamed, and then Mum waddled down from her room (the waddling is quite new, something to do with the baby pressing down between her legs, which I don't really want to think about), and then Dad came out of his study with the mad hair he gets when his writing is going badly, looking grumpy because he'd been interrupted, and even Twig left his comics, and it was impossible to get a sensible word out of anyone.

Whatever problem Zach had with our family, he has clearly got over it.

He came to find me later, before Zoran came round for dinner, when Flora was in the kitchen helping Mum and singing her head off. I was finishing *Jane Eyre* (and why does Mr Rochester have to be blind at the end, why?) when he turned up in my room and, not quite looking at me, said thank you for the letter.

'That's OK,' I said, not quite looking at him either. Then, because he was just hanging around in the doorway, I said, 'Do you want to sit down?' and he went and sat on my window seat.

'It's funny,' he said. 'First that video, then the letter. It's like you're writing my life for me.'

'I do want to be a writer,' I told him. 'And a filmmaker.'

'Well, I just wanted to say it really helped. The stuff about you all missing me, and being here and everything,' he said. Then he didn't speak for ages and I was wondering if it would be all right to go back to *Jane Eyre*, when he said, 'Just for the record, I never wanted to break up with Flora. I was really upset, but the reason I never called her was I threw my phone in the sea.'

'That was extreme,' I said.

'Mum wasn't answering my calls, and it just did my head in. So I threw it like a skimming stone. I made it bounce four times. It was kind of awesome.'

'I wish I'd seen it.'

Zach smiled that slow amazing smile that always reminds me why Flora likes him so much, except I think it was a little bit sadder than it used to be.

'Just don't tell Zoran,' he said. 'He doesn't know about it yet.'

'Have you heard from your mum at all?' I asked. 'Like on email or anything?'

Zach said he hadn't.

'I'm sorry,' I told him. 'Truly.'

For a moment, I thought he was going to confide something, but then he smiled and just said, 'Me too.'

'There you are, Zach!' Flora appeared at my door, still beaming. 'Mum wants ice cream, I have to go to the shop. Come with me!'

'We were talking!' I protested, but Zach was already on his feet, taking Flora's hand.

'Thanks again, Blue,' he said before he left.

'What for?' I heard Flora ask.

'Just stuff,' Zach replied, but he turned round when he got to the top of the stairs and gave me a little wink, like we both knew it was a lot more than just stuff.

Flora came into my room again after dinner, wafting in like some sort of fairy princess who hadn't stuffed herself with homemade pizza and brownies and ice cream all evening in between dragging her boyfriend out of the room to snog him under the impression no one else knew what she was doing. She draped herself over the end of my bed and hugged her knees to her chest, sighing.

'Did he tell you he threw his phone in the sea?' she said. 'Isn't that dramatic? That's the thing about Zach. He seems so quiet, but he's very passionate.'

I swear, drama is to Flora what blood is to a vampire.

'I told him about Scotland,' she burbled. 'Zach says distance doesn't matter. He says he'll come and visit me and we can explore the Highlands together. He says he's going to buy a motorbike.'

She drifted off to bed, and I went into the bathroom to brush my teeth. It's windy tonight, and even though the moon is full you can't always see it because of these big clouds rushing across the sky. I opened the window and the noise was so loud, with the trees in Chatsworth Square blowing and the wind whistling around me. The moon came out. I thought I saw the shadow of a person, not moving, still as a statue by the railings, and suddenly I thought of what Flora had said, how she thought Zach's mum had been watching her in the park, and I shivered.

I wonder what we would look like, if you were on the outside of our house, looking in. I wonder how it would feel.

The moon went back in and the shadow disappeared.

Monday 6 January

When I got to school this morning all everyone was talking about was how I assaulted Jake with a chocolate milkshake because he had two-timed me with an Australian surfer. All through morning school people kept saying things like 'Nice one, Blue,' sniggering and making milkshake-slurping noises.

'Man, I wish you'd recorded it,' Tom smirked. 'I'd pay money to watch it.'

Jake, who I thought would be mortified, has turned into a sort of minor celebrity. He looked really sheepish when he saw me this morning, in fact he went quite red, but in French when Rohan told him to '*déplacez-vous* out of my seat or *je vais jeter un* milkshake over *vous*', he laughed and high-fived him.

'Don't they have anything better to talk about?' I asked Dodi at break. It was freezing and most people stayed inside, but I made her sit in the playground so we wouldn't be interrupted. The boys were all playing football in the sports cage, but I kept us out of sight by hiding behind the music block.

'Better than you lobbing cold milky drinks around in cafes? I don't think so.'

Dodi is loving the reflected glory of being my best friend right at this moment. I wouldn't be surprised if she was going around telling people the whole thing was her idea in the first place.

'It's the best story they've had since Flora's YouTube video,' she said smugly. Then she got all businesslike. 'Actually, we need to talk. I left about two hundred messages on your stupid home answering machine last night.'

'Nobody ever listens to those,' I told her.

'Well you should. This is important. Guess what? It worked!'

'What are you talking about?' I asked.

'The milkshake throwing! Jake says you were brilliant. He says he never realised you cared so much.'

'I didn't do it to impress him,' I objected. 'It was a genuine act of anger.'

'He wants to get back together with you,' Dodi said. 'He rang me to ask what he should do. If you'd called me back like I asked you would know all this.'

'But Tallulah!' I said.

'Tallulah was a mistake,' Dodi said. 'Now he wants to be with you.'

'Well I don't want to be with him!' I cried. 'I can't believe you're even talking about this!'

Dodi said that Jake was really sorry, that he was almost crying on the phone, and that he really liked me.

'He's desperate for you to forgive him,' she said.

'He can't be that desperate. He's even laughing about the whole thing in a different language.'

Dodi said that was just Jake saving face. She said

Jake was too shy to talk to me about it himself, and she thought it was very brave of him to admit his mistakes. Jake behaved like an idiot, Dodi said, but he was basically a lovely person, and me and him were her favourite couple, and I should look out for Science, because she had heard rumours he was going to ask me to be his lab partner.

I did another thing today that I have never done before. I lied to the school nurse about having a headache and spent the whole of Science hiding in the sick room.

Tuesday 7 January

Now that we have sorted out the first of our problems, which was Flora and Zach, we have to deal with the second, which is Jas. After that, when everyone is happy again and I am free to live my life without the threat of imminent drowning in a lake of other people's tears, perhaps we can sort out what I'm supposed to do about Jake.

Zach and Jas's latest arrangement before he disappeared was this: because Jas is technically too young to perform – almost half the minimum required age – Zach is going to *pretend to be her* right up until the last moment, when he will stand to one side and she will slip on to the stage. She still won't be allowed to win, she says, but at least she will have made her point.

To say that Flora, who now knows everything, is happy with this arrangement is like saying Dad wasn't furious when he discovered Ron was using his favourite suede shoes as a toilet. Jas said at least he wasn't doing it on the carpet any more, but it didn't stop the shouting.

'Your name is *Jasmine*,' Flora said to Jas. 'It's a girl's name. And Zach is not a girl.'

'I registered as Jas,' Jas said. 'It could be short for Jason.'

Flora ignored her.

'It's bad enough you pretending you are nine,' she told Zach, 'without also making out that you are a girl.'

'I think you're missing the point,' I said, but she ignored me too.

'*I* will pretend to be Jas,' she declared. 'At least I'm the right gender.'

'I can't do it without Zach,' Jas said, and her voice was really shaky. I admit that at the start of this whole business I thought that two performance artists were more than one family could cope with, especially when you factor in Dad's artistic temperament and Mum's hormones as well, but when Jas said she couldn't do it without Zach I remembered how different she and Flora actually are.

'You don't have to do this,' I told her.

'Of course she does,' Flora said. 'She's started, hasn't she? She can't give up halfway through.'

The performance is in just over a week, and since Flora can't take to the stage in this particular role, she has appointed herself Director. She has given Jas five days to prepare, and then she has to perform in front of an audience.

'And be ready to receive constructive criticism,' Flora said.

'You scare me,' Zach said.

'Me too,' whispered Jas, but unlike Zach she wasn't laughing.

Friday 10 January

If Jas really was overlooked before – and personally I have my doubts about this – she certainly isn't any more, because the other thing Flora has insisted on is telling Mum and Dad.

'You clever, clever girl!' Mum (literally) cried, while Dad mumbled that he too was very proud and did we know that as a young man he also wrote poetry? Mum said we didn't need reminding and that for once this really wasn't about him, and then she asked Jas if many of her friends had entered the competition as well.

Flora may not have been completely honest about everything.

'The point is,' she said, 'it's Jas's big night, and we must all be there.'

Mum and Dad said they wouldn't miss it for the world. Jas looked like she might be sick. Mum made her soup and a hot-water bottle and told her she didn't have to go to school.

The person who doesn't get any attention in this family is not Jas, but me. And maybe Twig, but he enjoys it because it means he can impress Maisie with his babysitting skills without anyone asking where he is going. I, on the other hand, would welcome some advice because I am now being stalked by Jake. He has taken to leaving me notes saying things like 'I'm sorry' and 'Friends?' and 'I just want things to be like they were before'. Dodi denies all participation. If she's lying, which I'm pretty sure she is, it might be her putting the notes in my bag and coat pocket. If she really doesn't have anything to do with it, then Jake is finding a way of doing it, which is creepy.

Rehearsals for Jas's poetry recital are in full swing, which you would think the Dictator, I mean Director, would be happy about except she isn't, because Jas has refused to let Flora coach her and has insisted that Zach do it. 'He is *my* boyfriend,' Flora complained tonight after he and Jas disappeared upstairs to her room. 'She is completely monopolising him. Seriously, he is totally neglectful. I'm beginning to regret that I agreed to help.'

'When you say you agreed to help,' Twig said, 'did anyone actually ask you?'

I was tempted to add that Flora had no idea what it meant to have a neglectful boyfriend, except Zach had come downstairs again and was already making my point for me with a very extended goodnight kiss.

Until now Jas has refused to tell us anything at all about her poem, but tonight Flora beat it out of her, and I only just mean that metaphorically.

'If you don't tell me what you and Zach are up to,' Flora said, 'I will tell everyone, Mum, Dad and the organisers, that you are only nine years old.'

Twig said, surely Mum and Dad already knew that Jas was nine years old. Flora said he was really starting to get on her nerves this evening and whose side was he on? Jas said that while blackmail was despicable and Flora horrible, she was prepared to reveal her secret, which is that Zach has been helping her rehearse by setting her poem to music.

'What, that's it?' said Flora.

'Not setting exactly,' Jas went on. 'Zach says that he is helping me find the poem's rhythm. It's more that he helps me pick out the rhythms in the poem by playing them on his guitar. Then when I perform, I just have to imagine the music in my head. Zach says it is all to do with the inherent musicality of the text.'

We all just stared at her.

'Oh my God,' Flora said. 'Zach's created a monster.'

'Thank you,' said Jas.

Zoran says Zach is writing songs again. When he isn't helping Jas or snogging Flora or playing footie with Twig, he does the same as Jas and scribbles away in a corner. I asked what he was working on and Zoran said apparently it is completely different from his earlier work, which was very emotional and dark, and that he is trying to write a song that is perfectly happy but that this is much more difficult than you might think.

'It's about Flora,' Zoran said. We were sitting on the veranda, even though it was cold and nearly dark. Flora was hanging off the edge of the tree house with her sweatshirt riding up almost all the way to her bra. Zach was standing underneath her, looking up and grinning.

'Have you heard from his mum?' I asked and he said no, still nothing.

'What's happened to her?' I asked.

Zoran shrugged and said she had vanished again.

'And what about Mr Rudowski? Did you speak to him again?'

Zoran said yes he had, but he wasn't comfortable talking to me about it, because it was inappropriate.

'But I want to know,' I said.

'It's private, and it's not fair on Zach.'

I thought about this for a bit. 'I think it's not fair on Zach if you *don't* tell us,' I said at last. 'How else are we supposed to understand what he's going through?'

Zoran sighed. 'She's ill, Blue, and she's incredibly possessive of Zach. She hates to see him with other people, even though she's never around.'

'But I still don't understand . . .'

'People like that need help, but they don't always want it. It's hard for them and it's hard for the people around them. It killed Mrs Rudowska.'

'Wanda killed Zach's grandmother?'

'I didn't say that.' Zoran smiled faintly. 'I just meant that worrying about her daughter didn't help Mrs Rudowska's cancer. And now that's enough. I don't want to talk about it any more.'

Zoran looked exhausted. I gave him a nudge.

'He looks all right now,' I said, nodding at Zach gazing up at nearly naked Flora. Zoran laughed.

'I just have one last question,' I told him, and he groaned. 'Flora says Zach's mother was watching her when she was with Zach. And the other night, I thought I saw her outside the house. Don't you think that's weird?'

'I think that one day, with that imagination of yours, you're going to make a very fine writer,' Zoran said.

'No but seriously,' I said.

'Seriously. A great writer.'

He nudged me back, and I couldn't help laughing.

It was nice, sitting there and believing that.

The Film Diaries of Bluebell Gadsby

Scene Seven (Transcript)
Dress Rehearsal

INTERIOR. EVENING.

The Gadsby living room. Chairs are arranged in two neat rows upon which sit FLORA, ZACH, TWIG, DODI and ZORAN. All the lamps in the room have been assembled by the piano, where JASMINE stands in a pool of light, looking like the proverbial trapped bunny. The rest of the room is in darkness.
Applause.

> JAS
> Shall I start?

> FLORA
> Don't say 'Shall I start?' Survey
> the room and wait for silence.

Command our attention. Then, when you
have it, begin.

DODI
(whispering, to Twig)
How's it going with Maisie?

TWIG
(whispering back)
What's it to you?

DODI
(trying not to snigger)
Just that I heard she was hanging
out with Justin Murphy after school
last Wednesday.

TWIG
(a lot more loudly)
I heard you don't know how to mind
your own business.

ZORAN
(in a very loud stage whisper)
Please show respect to your sister
and be quiet.

                    JAS
               (to everyone)
    I actually don't see the point of
         this rehearsal at all.

                   FLORA
        SILENCE IN THE HOUSE, PLEASE!

                    JAS
            I can't do this.

                   ZACH
            Of course you can.

                    JAS
            I really can't.

Zach rises to whisper in her ear. Jas
gulps, nods, takes a deep breath and
tilts her chin as she turns back to
face the camera. She opens her mouth
to begin, but is put off by a scuffling
noise from behind the door.

                   TWIG
                (whispers)
    I bet that's the parents listening.

NOTE: Parents have been banned from the rehearsal on the grounds that grown-ups will only make Jas even more nervous.

Flora frowns and steps towards the door. The scuffling stops. Flora orders Jas to continue, but Jas is already at the door, which she flings open. PARENTS tumble into the room as Jas runs out. Zach, after a brief hesitation, goes after her. Flora starts to follow them, but he shakes his head and she remains.

Picture goes black.

The room stayed silent for about fifteen seconds and then it exploded.

'What were you *thinking*?' Flora yelled at the parents. 'You put her off the whole rehearsal!'

'It was your father's idea,' Mum mumbled. 'I didn't want to listen.'

'And yet there you were. Listening,' Flora pointed out.

'It's not fair to exclude us,' Dad declared.

I explained about adults making Jas nervous.

'Zoran's here!' Dad protested.

'He's not a real adult,' Flora said.

The whole point of filming was for Jas to watch herself afterwards and correct any mistakes. 'We'll have to do it again,' Flora said, but when Jas finally came back down, she just said no, she knew what was wrong and she was on it.

'No more rehearsals,' she said.

'But you're not ready . . .' Flora started to say, and then Zach wandered into the room with his guitar.

'Tell them,' Jas ordered.

'We're good,' Zach said, and that is when I knew that Zach is exactly the right boyfriend for Flora, because even though he doesn't shout and he's not particularly cool or tough like some of her previous boyfriends, all he has to do is shuffle into a room and say 'We're good' and she shuts up.

Zoran took me aside. 'You know she can't go through with this,' he said. 'Even if they don't disqualify her because of her age, they'll eat her alive.'

'She'll be fine,' I said.

'Unlike your parents, I do my research! She's a *child*, for God's sake! She's competing against adults. I don't approve of this secrecy. I've a good mind to tell them what's going on.'

'Jas is changing,' I said. 'If she has decided she wants to do this, no one can stop her.'

Wednesday 15 January

Today I found two red roses in my locker. Dodi admitted almost immediately that she had given Jake the combination to my lock.

'You have to stop encouraging him,' I told her.

'But he loves you so much!' she cried.

'This is getting ridiculous,' I said. 'When I like him, he doesn't like me. Now that I don't like him, he does like me. Why is that?'

Dodi said she didn't know, but that it was a shame, and maybe it was because opposites attract.

'So if I'm nice to him, he might go off me?' I asked.

'I still don't understand why you *want* him to go off you,' Dodi said. 'I think he's lovely.'

'Because he's ANNOYING!' I cried. 'And if you like him so much, why don't *you* go out with him?'

Dodi went a bit red and said, 'It's not me he likes,' and I felt mean because Dodi doesn't like to be reminded that she's never had a boyfriend.

'Well he's an idiot,' I said, and she cheered up a bit.

I thanked Jake for the flowers as we waited to go into Maths.

'It was very thoughtful of you,' I said. It was the first time I'd spoken to him since the Milkshake Incident, and his whole face lit up like it was on fire.

'Do you like them?' he asked.

'They're very pretty,' I said, and then I went to sit right at the back of the class by the window, where none of the teachers allow him to go.

'I'm coming to your sister's recital on Sunday!' he called out as Mr Maths came in.

'Whenever you're ready, Jake,' said Mr Maths.

Maybe my theory is wrong. Sometimes, if you're nice to people, it only makes them like you more.

Zach and Zoran were late. They were meant to meet us at home at half past six, but by quarter to seven Dad said we couldn't wait any longer. He phoned Zoran to tell him we were leaving. He also told him to get his act together because this was the most important night of his daughter's life and she needed all the support she could get.

'Stop being so jumpy,' Flora said. 'You're only making her more nervous.'

Dad said he couldn't help it. He said he felt responsible for Jas, because she must have inherited her writing genes from him. Mum reminded him that this wasn't about him.

'I'm sure there's a good reason for their lateness,' she added, but Dad still wouldn't calm down. 'They are selfish, thoughtless and incompetent,' he said as he tried to bundle us out of the house.

Twig announced Jas had just run upstairs to be sick.

The West London Poetic Society's Open Evening of Poetry took place in a church with salmon-pink walls and dark green woodwork and paintings of angels in gold and blue above the altar, which sounds hideous but wasn't, as I had plenty of time to observe through what for the most part was a long, dull evening. The first thing I noticed when we went in was how big it was. Also, how many people in West London appeared to like poetry, and how old everyone was compared to Jas. I don't think I ever realised how young nine was before tonight. A lot of the people in the room looked like our next-door neighbours, Mr and Mrs Bateman, who are way past sixty and wear beige and do a lot of gardening, or else they were people Mum and Dad's age in long colourful shawls and no make-up who looked as though they might like to walk barefoot through fields on beautiful dewy mornings chanting hymns of praise to the sunrise. There was a man in his twenties pacing up and down waving his arms doing some last-minute rehearsal, and a girl wearing a nose ring and a yellow jumpsuit who looked a bit confused, but there was absolutely nobody as small and terrified as Jas.

'Tickets are ten pounds each,' said a lady in a maroon dress with long grey hair and no bra. 'Are you here to support one of the acts?'

'Where are all the other children?' asked Mum.

The ticket lady looked baffled, but we'd rehearsed this. Flora took control. 'Jas Gadsby,' she said to the ticket lady, and at the same time she turned towards the parents. 'Dad, why don't you give me the money for the tickets and take Mum to sit down?'

'You do look tired, Mum,' said Twig.

'Let me help you,' I offered as Flora reached into Dad's pocket for his wallet.

'Well come along, young star!' Dad draped his arm around Jas's shoulders. 'Where do the performers sit?' he asked.

'Anywhere near the front.' The ticket lady still looked puzzled.

Jas took her seat in a daze and said she was going to be sick again.

'Keep it in, shrimp,' said Flora when she joined us. 'This is your big night.'

'I still don't understand why there aren't any other children,' Mum said.

'Your boyfriend's here, by the way,' Flora smirked at me.

'I don't have a boyfriend,' I said.

'Tell him that. He's sitting two rows back.'

I sneaked a look and it was true. Just across the aisle, two rows back, Jake and Dodi were sitting together. Dodi beamed. Jake gave a little wave then blushed scarlet. I turned back round to the front.

'I'm going to kill her,' I muttered. 'I didn't think he would actually come.'

Flora snorted.

Zoran slid on to the end of our bench just as the lights were dimming.

'Where have you *been*?' Flora asked. For all her stomping about, she was almost as nervous as Jas.

'Everything's fine,' Zoran said.

'And where is Zach?'

'He *is* coming, isn't he?' Jas whispered.

'I'm here.' Zach slid in next to Zoran, who put his arm around his shoulders.

'All right, mate?' I heard him ask.

'Yeah, fine,' Zach answered. Zoran squeezed him and let him go.

'Do we have to be so squashed up?' asked Twig.

I feel a little sad writing it, because I hate to give up on anything, but I'm not sure poetry will ever be my thing. The long-haired brightly shawled ladies came and went, along with the grey-haired beige cardigan-wearing older people. The young man in the business suit cried as he recited a poem written when his wife got married for the second time. 'Not to me,' he added in case we hadn't understood why he was sad.

'This *isn't* a children's competition!' Mum remarked. Dad gulped and looked like *he* was going to be sick.

'Jas will be absolutely fine,' Zoran said firmly.

The girl in the yellow jumpsuit must have realised she was in the wrong place and vanished without a trace. Twig and I both fell asleep and were woken by Flora with a sharp elbow in the ribs because the compère had just called out Jas's name and she was rising from her seat, white as a ghost and shaking like a leaf, staring at the front of the church with Zach standing next to her holding his guitar.

'Ready?' he mouthed. Jas tried to smile.

'Jas Gadsby!' The compère called again, and Jas and Zach walked down the aisle together, Jas in her usual uniform of black dress and leggings and silver high tops and Zach with his guitar on his back.

'I don't understand,' the compère frowned when they reached the front.

'Neither do I,' murmured Dad.

Flora sighed as Zach reached out to take Jas's hand.

Jas suddenly seemed to grow about six inches and took the microphone.

'Just because I am nine years old', she announced, 'does not mean I can't write poetry.'

A lot of people started to laugh. Dad put his head in his hands. Zach smiled, stepped on to the stage and began to play. Jas stood very still at the front of the stage looking tiny, waited for the audience to be silent, and began:

'There is a gravestone where I like to sit . . .
A stony relic of one long dead.
Something about it seems to fit
The creature that lives inside my head.

'She's good!' Dad breathed.

'It rhymes,' Twig whispered.

'Shut up, both of you,' Flora hissed.

Jas went on, Zach still strumming softly along with her.

'Around the graveyard the city roars,
The steady beat of human living.
Deep inside a creature claws,
A creature who is not forgiving.

'This creature belongs to the night,
This creature shies away from light,
This creature must keep out of sight
Who lives inside my head.

'The grave is strewn with moss and flowers.
Here birds can sometimes come to nest.
I sit here often and for hours.
Here the beast inside me likes to rest.'

I know I'm biased and also that I slept through a lot of the others, but Jas's number was the best by far. She and Zach repeated the *This creature belongs to the night* verse several times together, like a chorus, so it sounded more like a song than a poem, and maybe that, as well as it being Zach and Jas, is why I liked it. But I wasn't the only one. There was a moment's stunned silence at the end, because I'm not sure the audience were expecting something quite so dark from one so young, but then they were all on their feet, cheering. A journalist from the local paper was trying to take photographs and write in his notebook at the same time. Jas beamed and hugged Zach, who grinned and hugged her back. Dad yelled, 'That's my daughter! That's my daughter!' punching the air with his fist, Twig and Flora and I jumped up and down on our seats to get a better look, Zoran held Mum as she cried her eyes out. Behind us I could hear Dodi and Jake cheering too.

'She was amazing!' Dodi yelled when I turned around.

'Amazing!' Jake echoed. I forgot about him being creepy and waved.

A lot of the time my family drive me mad, but tonight wasn't like that. Tonight was absolutely brilliant.

She didn't win, of course, just as Zoran said she wouldn't. First prize went to one of the shawled ladies for a sonnet about cats, and the second prize went to one of the old men for a ballad about the love of his life being like a vampire, which made the young man in the suit cry even more. Afterwards, just before the local journalist asked to take a photograph of all of us, the competition organisers gave Mum and Dad and Jas a long lecture about all the rules she had broken, and how she had abused their trust by entering false details, and how this disqualified her from winning. 'But your work shows promise,' the lady organiser said, with what I think was the most patronising smile I have ever seen. 'I am sure you will mature into a very interesting young poet.'

Flora blew a raspberry behind her back. We all laughed. Gloria and Bill turned up, Bill still looking like a tramp, Gloria stunning in head-to-toe tight-fitting black. She told Jas her poetry was even better than her riding and Jas beamed even more. Dad and Zoran both gaped at Gloria. Twig sniggered. The local reporter took our photograph and we all spilled out of the church into the night. Zach lifted Jas on to his shoulders and she screeched for him to put her down, but she was still laughing.

Flora stood on tiptoe to kiss him on the lips. Mum leaned on Dad's arm, and they were both laughing.

It was brilliant.

And then everything changed.

The stone caught Mum just above her right temple. She stumbled, slipped and crashed to the ground. Someone screamed, I still don't know who. Jas tumbled down from Zach's shoulders, but he caught her in his arms before she hit the pavement. A man pushed through the crowd of people coming out of the church, saying he was a doctor, and knelt beside Mum, who was lying with her head in Dad's lap.

'I'm all right,' Mum murmured. Her head was bleeding.

'My wife is pregnant!' Dad cried.

The doctor leaned over to take Mum's pulse. For a minute, because he smiled at her, I thought everything was going to be all right. Then he looked at Dad and told him to call an ambulance.

Sunday 19 January (the middle of the night)

No one saw who did it, but I know. And I'm not the only one.

It's so obvious.

Dad went to the hospital in an ambulance with Mum last night, while Zoran drove us home in our car. Zach sat with him in the front, with Flora and the others in the row behind them. I sat in the back.

Jas was crying and asking questions. 'Why would anyone do that? Why Mummy? Why here, why tonight, why now?'

'I don't know,' Flora answered.

I thought about the baby, the feel of its head under my hand on Mum's tummy, the jab when it kicks, Mum saying, 'Imagine how it feels for me?' Mum on Christmas Day, snoring on the sofa, and playing charades on Boxing Day. I wanted to say something but I couldn't speak. Literally. It was like the connection between my brain and my mouth was broken.

If anything happens to them . . . I clenched my fists till my nails dug into my palms. If I wasn't writing this, I'd still be clenching them now.

'Who would do that?' Jas sobbed, and Flora said again that she didn't know. But I know, and Zoran knows, and Zach knows, who threw the stone at Mum.

Neither of them talked the whole way home, but at one point Zoran reached out to squeeze Zach's shoulder again, like he did before. I was too far away to hear what he said but it sounded like a question. Zach shrugged and looked out of the window. He looked like he wanted to cry, and I thought, good.

I wish we'd never met him and his stupid mother. I wish Zoran had never agreed to look after him.

Zoran dropped Zach off first before taking us home, and then he said he'd stay with us until Dad got back. Flora told him he didn't have to, but he said he wanted to.

We didn't go to bed. Instead we brought our duvets down to the living room, where we huddled together on the sofa and waited. It was past two when Dad got home. Everybody was asleep except me and Zoran, sitting together in the dark, still not talking. Dad sat down with us on the sofa. The others woke up and we all crawled over to him.

'How's Mum?' Twig asked.

'All right, but they're keeping her under observation.'

'What about the baby?' asked Flora.

'We'll know more tomorrow.'

I pressed in closer to him. I was vaguely aware of a hand on my shoulder, Zoran murmuring, 'I'll call in the morning.' I thought he might tell Dad then, but he didn't say a word, and neither did I.

We all went upstairs, but once the others were in bed I crept back down again. I found Dad in his study, sitting at his desk with his head in his hands, surrounded by papers.

'I thought I'd try to work,' he said. 'I knew I wouldn't be able to sleep.'

I moved a stack of books from the armchair in the corner and curled up in it.

'How is your book going?' I asked. Badly, Dad said. Then he said that it hardly mattered any more.

'I swear to God, if anything happens to them ...' His voice was shaking. He pressed his hands down on his desk, like doing that was the only thing stopping him from throwing everything on the floor or ripping up all those precious sheets of paper.

'I know,' I said.

'If anything happens to your mother or that baby,' he said in a steadier voice, 'I will find the person who did this thing and I will make him pay. I will rip him to pieces. I will tear off his head ...'

'Dad,' I said.

'I will pull out his heart and stamp on his guts and ...'

'Dad, you're scaring me!'

He was prowling around his study now, punching his right fist into the palm of his left hand. He stopped right in front of me and looked at me like he hadn't seen me properly until then.

'I'll kill him,' he said.

I can't talk to him when he's like this. I spoke to Flora instead. I found her sitting on her bed with her arms wrapped round her knees, staring at her phone. I sat next to her, but she didn't look up.

'I think it was Zach's mother,' I whispered.

She carried on staring at her phone.

'It has to be,' I insisted. 'Who else would do something like that? She's mad, Flora. Zoran says she killed her own mother.'

'Zach's gran died of cancer.'

'You saw her in the park,' I went on. 'Remember? I've seen her too, I'm sure I have. She's been watching us, Flora, she's jealous and she hates us.'

'I'm not even sure it was her I saw,' Flora said tonelessly. 'And even if I did, it doesn't mean anything. It's not proof.'

'Flora, Mum's in hospital!'

She looked up at last, and I saw that she had been crying. 'Does it matter?' she asked. 'You heard what Dad said, Mum's all right. I don't want to fight with Zach again.'

'So you do think it was her!'

She didn't answer for ages.

'We have to do something,' I said. 'What if she does it again?'

'I don't want to talk about it.'

She lay down and pulled the duvet over her head. I waited for her to say something else, but she didn't and I left her too.

I don't know what to do.

Monday 20 January

I'm writing this from Zoran's front doorstep. None of us went to school today.

The police came this morning. There were two of them, a man who didn't look like we interested him very much at all and a woman who kept calling us 'dear'. They said they were sorry to intrude on us when we must be so preoccupied but they just had a few questions and perhaps the younger children would rather not be present? The way they said it made it obvious they were the ones who had much rather Jas and Twig weren't there.

'If there is to be a police investigation,' Twig said, 'there is absolutely no way I will not be present.'

'Me neither,' Jas whispered. They had been standing by the door but now Jas took Twig's hand

and led him to the sofa, where they sat together, very close, and didn't let go. The policewoman smiled, like she thought they were impossibly cute. The policeman didn't.

Dad stood by the door with his coat on, looking anxious.

Flora sat in the red armchair in her tartan pyjama bottoms and the old cardigan she always wears when she's worried or upset, concentrating really hard on trying to answer the police's questions. She didn't look at me.

I thought, I have to tell them. Mum is lying in hospital, and I have to tell them what I know. But Flora was talking, saying we had no idea who could have done it and I thought, she's right, thinking something isn't proof. Last night I *thought* I knew, but that's not the same thing. And the longer Flora talked, the harder it got to say anything.

Our mother had no enemies, said Flora. None of us were aware of any quarrels or arguments she may have had, and nobody saw what happened.

At the end, the policewoman said they would do their best to find the culprit, but that it sounded like a random attack and that unless he struck again the attacker would be difficult to catch. She said that someone from Victim Support would be in touch to offer counselling. Dad said that would be great but the person who needed support right now was his wife with their unborn child, and then he pretty much ran out of the house to go to the hospital.

Jas started to cry again.

I love Dad, but I wish he was better in a crisis.

After Dad and the police had gone, I waited for Flora to say something to me, but she still didn't. And then I thought, I don't care what she thinks, and I came here. Zoran is out. It's half past twelve, and I've been sitting on this doorstep for nearly an hour. Luckily it's mild again, and sunny. There's this big tree outside Zoran's building, and the squirrels in it are going crazy, chasing each other round and round the trunk. There's a robin too, hopping about making chirping noises, and a fat old tabby cat sleeping on the wall in the sun. It seems quite incredible to me that all this is going on when Mum is lying in hospital.

Zoran just turned in from the street. Time to stop writing.

I'm clenching my fists again.

I'm in bed now. Dad called from the hospital this evening. Mum and the baby are both fine, but the doctors still want to keep her in for a few days just in case. He explained that she has been suffering from very high blood pressure and the doctors had worried that it might be something called pre-eclampsia. It isn't, which is a good thing because we looked it up on Google and the only cure is to deliver the baby, and if that happened it could die because it is still so small.

'I don't want the baby to die.' Jas began to cry and Twig looked like he might too.

'No one is going to die,' I said.

'What if it happens again!' Jas wailed. 'What if there's a murderer stalking her! What if someone is trying to kill her!'

The Jas who tears round obstacle courses on horseback and recites poetry to a packed audience has completely vanished.

'Nobody is stalking us,' I said, but what if that's not true?

Zoran went to see Mr Rudowski this morning. That's where he was when I was waiting for him on his doorstep, and that's why he didn't call us this morning like he said he would.

'Where's Zach?' I asked. Zoran said he was back at school. He said it was important to keep things as normal as possible.

'What news of Cassie and the baby?' he asked. I didn't answer.

'The police came,' I said instead. 'Speaking of normal.'

Zoran was looking for his keys, and he didn't look at me.

'What did they say?' he asked.

'They wanted to know if Mum had enemies. Flora said no. I wanted to say yes, but I couldn't, because I wasn't sure.'

'You weren't sure of what?'

'If Mum has enemies.' And then I didn't know how to say what I wanted to say and we'd reached the top of the stairs and were going into Zoran's flat, and I wondered what Grandma or Dodi would do if it was them and I just blurted out, 'Was it Zach's mother who did it?'

Sometimes when you don't know how to do something it's easier to pretend you're someone else.

Zoran sighed and said yes, he thought it was.

I didn't know what to say next, and I suppose

Zoran didn't either, because he just stood there leaning against a wall with his arms crossed, looking at the floor and frowning.

'She came back just before the show,' he said at last. 'We left the house and she was waiting for us outside. She was upset. She'd finally been to the hospital to see her father and they had a fight.'

'What was the fight about?'

Zoran said Wanda wouldn't say, but Mr Rudowski told him this morning that the fight was about money. To put it bluntly, Mr Rudowski said, Wanda was in trouble and she came back to get what she could before he died.

'That's horrible,' I said, and Zoran agreed but said that there was nothing like the possibility of imminent death of close relatives to bring out the worst in people.

'But if she just came back for the money, why did she want to see Zach?'

Zoran's face softened for a moment. 'He's her son, Blue.'

'But she's horrible to him.'

'I didn't say she was logical. I just said he's her son. She's confused but she still loves him. Just as he loves her. He was so sweet with her, Blue. Put his arm round her, tried to calm her down. She was hysterical, kept saying her father had sent her away again – nothing at all about the money, obviously. Zach said he couldn't let Jas down, and asked her to come with us. He told her he'd love that. He even asked me if she could stay with us.'

'But she didn't.'

'Of course not. She started crying that Zach didn't love her any more, that she'd lost everything and that it was all his and her father's fault. And then she must have followed us and waited for us to come out. You know what happened next.'

Zoran said that he had wanted to tell Dad last night but Zach had begged him not to, and given what Zach had just been through and what he'd done for Jas, he agreed to wait. And then this morning he decided to go and see Mr Rudowski.

'What did he say?' I asked.

'He begged me not to go to the police.'

'But she hurt Mum! Doesn't he care?'

'She's his daughter,' Zoran said gently. 'And what are the police going to do?'

'Catch her!'

'She needs medical help, Blue.'

'But what about Mum? What if Wanda comes back and attacks her again?'

Zoran said that he would find her. He said he

would never let anything bad happen to any of us, and that was why his biggest priority now was to make sure Wanda got the help she needed from doctors and from her own family.

'We have to tell Dad,' I said.

Zoran hesitated. 'If that's what you want.'

'Of course it's what I want! Why wouldn't we tell Dad?'

'He has a lot on his plate right now. And David can get a bit – irrational himself. I wonder if we might wait. For Zach's sake.'

I thought about Dad last night, how angry he was.

'If you want to do the right thing by one person,' I said, 'does it always mean you are doing the wrong thing by somebody else?'

Zoran said sometimes that was the case, but not always.

'Flora knows,' I told him. 'But she won't admit it. She says I'm imagining things, but really she's afraid of upsetting Zach.'

'Let me find Wanda,' Zoran said.

Jas is sleeping with Twig tonight. I just stopped in Flora's room on my way back from the bathroom. She hasn't asked me where I went this afternoon, and I haven't told her.

We went to the hospital today. Mum is on a ward with four other women. Her window looks out over the railway tracks and her bed is separated from the others by curtains. She says it's super cosy and all the women chat to each other and swap stories, but she looks exhausted.

Maybe Flora is feeling guilty for her silence, because she flitted about Mum's cubicle arranging flowers and plumping pillows and feeding her soup she brought from home in a Thermos like she was the sort of nurse you see in black-and-white films who looks like a nun.

I read out loud to her from *Jane Eyre*.

Twig told us about the trains he could see out of the window.

Jas sat on the floor because there weren't enough chairs, hugging her knees and looking sorrowful. I got to the bit where Jane traipses across the moors, lost and abandoned without a hope in the world, and she started to sniff. Twig stared at her, amazed.

'Are you crying because of the book?' he asked. 'Because I think it's the stupidest thing I ever heard.'

'You're just uncultured,' I told him.

'Let's not quarrel,' Flora murmured, and Jas howled even louder.

I asked her, 'Are you really crying because of *Jane Eyre*?' and she gave a giant hiccough and wailed that NO, OF COURSE SHE WASN'T, and then she threw herself on Mum's bed shouting MUMMY MUMMY MUMMY and that it was all her fault. Mum said no no no of course it wasn't and Jas said yes yes yes it was, until a nurse came along and kicked us out, telling us we'd be the death of our mum if we carried on like that, which really didn't help at all.

Jake came round this afternoon. He turned up on the doorstep with a bag full of chocolate bars and before I could even open my mouth to talk he said, 'I just wanted to say I'm sorry about your mum,' and I let him in. I wasn't sure what I should do with him so we sat on the stairs eating the chocolate while I told him what I could, which wasn't very much.

'It was such an awesome evening,' Jake said. 'Until, you know, the attack and everything. Jas and the poetry and Flora's boyfriend, it was brilliant.'

I couldn't help smiling. Jake is basically inarticulate, but I always know what he means, and he's right. Jas and the poetry and Jake *were* brilliant. Then I wished I *hadn't* smiled, because he gazed at me, all hopeful, like he thought my smile meant something completely different.

'I really like you, Blue,' he said.

I couldn't think of a single thing to say. All I could think about was Mum and how she looked this afternoon and Jas screaming MUMMY MUMMY MUMMY as the nurse pushed us out of the room.

'I'm really sorry about Tallulah,' Jake went on. 'I don't know what I was thinking. I think I went a bit crazy, remembering the beach and surfing and stuff. Like even though we were back in England it wasn't real life, you know?'

He looked so sorry for himself I almost started to feel sorry for him too. I love Jake in a way, I really do, but he does pick his moments to try and get philosophical.

'Can't we try again?' he asked. 'You're one of my best friends, Blue. I hate that we don't talk any more.'

'You're one of my best friends too, Jake,' I said, and he beamed.

'That thing you did with the milkshake was wicked,' he said. 'I mean, you kind of ruined my hoody and everything, but the way you just *did* it was mad. It was like you couldn't care less what I thought.'

Boys are so strange.

'So are we back together and everything?' Jake asked. I told him, all I said was he was one of my best friends too, and he said yeah, I know, but that meant something, right?

I figure there are enough miserable people in the world. Why add to them unnecessarily? And maybe it would be nice to go out with Jake again. Maybe this time, if I didn't expect too much from it, it could work.

'I'll think about it,' I said.

Jake said that was awesome.

'You'd better go now,' I said. Jake said OK, and asked if I was coming back to school tomorrow. He leaned towards me but I moved away. I'm really not in the mood for more kissing practice.

'You can leave the chocolate,' I said as he went to pick up the bag.

Flora says I am making a big mistake. She swooped down on the chocolate from the first-floor landing the minute Jake was gone. She was listening to every word we said. She says when it comes to boys, you have to let them know exactly where they stand at all times and that it's only inviting trouble if you don't. She says that in the long run, it's kinder to be cruel.

She still hasn't said a word about Zach's mum.

Jas announced this morning that she had had nightmares all night.

'It's true,' Twig said. 'She came and slept with me again.'

I glared at Flora. She looked away.

I called Zoran last night, but they still haven't heard from Wanda.

On the way home from school today, Dodi repeated that she was tired of leaving messages on the house phone that no one ever answers.

'Either you buy a new phone,' she said, 'or we get the old one back from Mme Gilbert.'

'Mme Gilbert hates me,' I said, and then I switched off because Dodi started saying how the reason she called me last night was to talk about Jake, and I'm not comfortable discussing Jake right now. I think Flora may have been right about needing to be more clear. This morning there was another rose pinned to my locker, and during Maths he gave me a drawing of a little dog wagging its tail and looking hopeful. I'd forgotten how good he is at drawing, but seriously, a little dog?

'You're not listening,' Dodi said. She gave me this

really sharp look, a bit like Grandma, and said, 'Tell me everything.'

'I'm not sure I'm allowed to,' I said.

'Forget *that*!' she snorted.

'I *can* sort of understand Flora not wanting to stir things up with Zach,' she admitted when I'd finished. We were at home now, carrying tea up to my bedroom and talking in whispers. 'He seems to be pretty protective of his mum. And I guess if *your* mum's OK . . .'

'It's not right,' I said. 'It's like she's more loyal to Zach than to Mum. And also, what if Zach's mother does it again? Zoran says he's going to find her, but he hasn't. We *have* to tell the police.'

Dodi whispered that she thought I was probably right. Then, because she can never be serious for very long, she nudged me, nearly making me spill my tea.

'I'll say one thing for Jake,' she grinned. 'However useless he is as a boyfriend, at least his mum isn't a known criminal. She might be a bit boring, but she's definitely not the rock-slinging type.'

'It's not funny,' I told her, but Dodi nudged me again, and I started to smile. 'It's not a great recommendation for a boyfriend though, is it?' I said, and she agreed that the fact that Jake's mum didn't hurl stones at people probably wasn't enough of a reason to go out with him. And then we were going into my room, and Dodi jumped and this time the tea did go all over the carpet as she yelled, 'WHAT ARE YOU *DOING?*' at Jas who was standing on my bed like a little ball of fury holding my diary and waving it above her head screaming, 'You knew! You knew and you didn't say!'

'Give that back!' I cried, but she backed up against the wall, holding it behind her.

'I heard you!' she shouted. 'You were talking about it with *Dodi*!'

'Calm down, titch,' Dodi said. 'I'm her BFF.'

'I'm going to tell Daddy!' Jas screamed. She made a run for the door, but Dodi caught her. Jas tried to bite her, but Dodi is surprisingly strong.

'Dad's at the hospital.' I tried to keep very calm, even though I was shaking.

'Then I'll phone him!' Jas shouted. 'I'll run away! I'll tell the police!'

'Tell the police what?' Flora wandered into my room. 'Why is Dodi holding Jas? What is Jas screaming about? What on earth is going on?'

'She'll come back,' Jas insisted. 'It's all here in Blue's book. She's mad and she hates Mum and Zoran can't do anything to stop her!'

'What are you talking about?' Flora repeated.

'She killed her own mother!' Jas wailed. 'And now she wants to kill ours.'

Flora looked at me. I shrugged, and told Jas to give her my diary.

It was weird, watching Flora read. It was like she stopped breathing, like a balloon with a tiny puncture, getting smaller and smaller until she was almost completely flat.

'Why didn't you tell me you'd spoken to Zoran?' she said when she'd finished.

'You didn't want to hear,' I said.

Jas said, 'I'm really scared, Flora.'

And even though Flora's loyalties may be divided, she's still our big sister. She started to breathe again and held her hand out to Jas.

'Come on,' she said. 'I think it's time to have a chat with Zach.'

Wednesday 22 January (much later)

I'm so tired I can barely hold my pen.

Dodi left us on the way to Zoran's flat. She may not be the most tactful person in the world, but I think even she realised that she might get in the way. Flora marched down the street in silence, still holding Jas's hand. I don't know what she was thinking as she walked, but she looked more and more angry with every step.

'It's me,' Flora snapped at the intercom when Zoran answered, and then she stomped up the stairs. Zoran was waiting on the landing. He didn't even say hello. He took one look at Flora and stepped aside to let us in. Flora stormed straight into the living room.

'Stay with Blue,' she ordered Jas, who transferred her hand from Flora's to mine.

The way Flora barrelled into that room, I thought she was going to yell and scream and try doing some of the things Dad said he wanted to do, the ripping and stamping and punching stuff. She looked like some warrior queen about to dismember invading hordes, but then Zach turned round from the window where he was standing and she stopped dead in her tracks.

Zach looks dreadful. Not just like a bit sad or worried or depressed, but truly horrible. The purple smudges under his eyes are almost black, his eyes are darker than ever and his skin is so pale he looks like he might be dead. He was actually a bit scary, and I know Jas thought so too because she moved closer so she was standing right up against me, but that was not the effect he had on Flora.

The effect he had on Flora was that she gasped, then held her arms out and rushed towards him, crying, 'Baby, what's happened to you!'

'I'm sorry,' Zach said. 'Zoran told me you knew. I'm so, so sorry about what she did. I should have said something.'

'No, *I* should have said something!' Flora said. 'I guessed, but I didn't want to upset you. I shouldn't have left you all alone.'

Then she threw her arms around him and showered his face in kisses.

'It's not her fault,' Zach said when Flora finally let him breathe again and we were all sitting around Zoran's tiny coffee table. 'She gets so jealous. I should have seen it coming.'

'Of course it's not your fault!' Flora cried. She started kissing him again.

I glanced at Zoran, who was frowning, looking worried. Jas moved even closer to me and whispered, 'Ask him where she is now,' but I had another question first.

'If she gets so jealous of you, why did she go away?' I asked. 'Before, I mean, not just after Christmas.'

'Leave him alone, Blue,' Flora said.

'It's a valid question,' Zoran murmured.

'It was Grandpa,' Zach said. 'Their fight, after Grandma died. He didn't give her a choice.'

'She was always lovely when she came back,' Zach insisted. 'She does crazy things sometimes, but she's not a bad person. And she knew Gran was there to look after me. She wouldn't have left me if I hadn't had Gran.'

I thought about Grandma, then. Once when we were staying with her, the vet came to see one of her ponies, who was lame. The vet said the pony should be put down. 'There isn't really a choice,' the vet said, but instead Grandma nursed the pony back to health. No one can ever ride him again, but Grandma says at least he's happy, living quietly in her paddock.

'There's always a choice,' Grandma said.

I didn't say anything now, because it didn't seem right, but I thought it.

Jas tugged at my arm. I caught Flora's eye. She nodded, like she was saying 'you do it', and laced her fingers through Zach's.

So much for the protective big sister.

'The reason we came,' I said, 'is that Jas is worried . . .'

'Not *just* me,' Jas said.

'. . . is that we're *all* worried in case Wanda, I mean your mum, attacks *our* mum again.'

'You're going to find her, aren't you Zach?' said Flora.

'He hasn't found her so far,' I pointed out.

'But he will,' she replied.

Zoran crouched down in front of Jas. 'I promise nothing bad is going to happen again,' he said. 'But just so you feel really safe, shall we go and tell your dad everything?'

'And call the police?' said Jas.

'If that's what he wants to do.' He glanced over at Zach. 'I'm sorry, but this has gone far enough,' he said. 'Cassie and the baby might be out of danger, but I'm not having Jas going around frightened.'

The house felt different when we got home. Dad had put the heating right up, and there was a big bunch of flowers on the table in the hall. 'Mummy's flowers from the hospital!' Jas cried. 'She's back!'

She ran upstairs. Flora and I followed. Mum was lying in bed, looking tired but happy in her old pink dressing gown, with a cup of tea and a plate of biscuits on a tray, Twig, Ron and Hermione lying beside her, and Dad beaming over them, wearing an apron and looking surprisingly like an old mother hen.

'You're better!' Jas flung herself on to the bed. Mum laughed and reached out to hug her.

I always knew Dad would react badly. After we'd all hugged Mum, Flora said Zach and Zoran were downstairs. Mum said they should come up. 'After all,' Mum said, 'they are part of this family too.' Zach and Zoran came in, looking nervous. Zoran explained.

'I'm sorry,' Zoran said. 'I should have said something earlier. It's just . . . It's been difficult.'

Mum put her hand on his arm. 'Dear Zoran, you're not telling me anything I didn't already suspect.'

My mum's amazing.

Zoran pressed his forehead against her hand and murmured, 'Thank you.'

'The thing to do now is find her.' Mum reached out to Zach. 'You poor thing, you look so tired.'

And it could have ended there, except that's when Dad shouted, 'No!'

Everyone turned to look at him. 'No, no, no!' he repeated. 'You all knew and you never said anything? Blue knew, and Flora knew, and Zoran knew, and you knew, and nobody thought to tell me? I have spent days *out of my mind* with worry, worried about how to keep my family safe, and NOBODY THOUGHT TO TELL ME? I'm calling the police.'

'No, David.' Mum repeated what Zoran had said to me, that there was no point.

Jas whimpered. 'Don't be scared,' I whispered to her. 'You can see Mum isn't.'

'I knew you'd react like this,' Mum told Dad. 'That's why I didn't tell you. You were so worried.'

'Me too,' I said. 'I'm sorry, Daddy.'

'I thought you might stop me seeing Zach,' Flora said.

Zach, speaking for the first time, said, 'I'm really, really sorry, Mr Gadsby.'

Flora really should have learned by now not to put ideas into Dad's head. Dad looked from Flora to Zach and back at Flora again, and said, 'Well you were right, that's exactly what I am going to do. You two are not to see each other.'

Mum said, 'David, that hardly seems fair,' and Dad said he didn't care about being fair, and was he the only one here to appreciate the full gravity of the situation? 'That woman is still on the loose,' he said, not noticing Zach flinch. 'And she is a danger to my family.'

'But it's not Zach's fault!' Flora protested.

'I don't care!' Dad roared.

'Daddy!'

'He's right, Flora,' said Zach. I wouldn't have thought it was possible, but he looked even paler than before.

'But it's not your fault!' Flora repeated. She squared her shoulders and faced Dad. 'You can't stop me! I'm seventeen years old and . . .'

Dad held up his hand to silence her. 'Zach, you are a gentleman,' he said. 'And now, if you all don't mind, I am going for a walk.'

He was very dignified as he left the room. I slipped out after him and asked him if he would like company on his walk, but he said, still dignified, that he would rather be alone. He walked down the stairs with his head held high. In the hall, he put on his coat, his scarf and his old trilby. He slipped out of his indoor shoes and pulled on his trainers.

'AGGGGGGGGhhhhhhhhhhhhhhhhhhh!'

I swear his scream made the house shake, and his swearing afterwards would have made a pirate blush.

Apparently Ron had been using his shoes as a toilet again.

'Those ******* ****** cats!' Dad yelled. He pulled

off his trainers and hurled them out into the street. Tore down to the basement for some clean socks. Stormed back upstairs, put on the socks, and his shoes, and walked out slamming the door.

Dinner was silent. Dad made pasta with a jar of puttanesca sauce and even though Jas hates olives, she ate the whole thing without complaining. Mum stayed in bed. Flora stayed in her room. Ron and Hermione stayed in the shed.

Friday 24 January

Flora skipped school today to see Zach. He called her late last night to ask her to meet him, and she asked me to cover for her. She said, looking more serious than I have ever seen her, not to ask any questions but that things had changed since Wednesday. We left home together this morning as usual, but after we'd dropped Jas and Twig at school we went off in separate directions.

I went to the school office to tell them Flora was sick.

She went to spend the day with Zach and his mother.

She told me everything this afternoon when she got back.

Zach finally heard from his mum last night. She said she wanted to see him, and he thought it would be good for Flora to go too.

Flora said, 'But what if she attacks me?' and Zach said that wasn't going to happen, and that he wanted his mum to see how great Flora was.

'Once she knows you a bit, she'll love you,' Zach said.

'That was a bit deluded,' I remarked, and Flora agreed, but she went anyway.

She met him at the Tube station and they walked down to the river hand in hand. 'Does she know I'm coming?' Flora asked and Zach replied, 'Yes, of course, and she thinks it's a really good idea.'

It was a beautiful day. They walked past a little park and some pubs and a houseboat with a dog on the roof and a woman watering pot plants and it was all really pretty except Flora was too nervous to enjoy it. They came to a tiny street with gardens on one side and gardens giving on to the river on the other, and Zach finally stopped in front of a big house with black and white marble steps going up to a dark red door and said, 'Well, this is where I live, this is my grandparents' house.'

'What was it like?' I asked.

'The house? Old, a bit like a museum. Old furniture, and old books, and a kitchen which reminds me of Grandma's, except not as big. Loads of photographs of Zach and his gran. Only one of him and Wanda. But we didn't stay long. Zach called out for his mum and she didn't answer, so he said maybe she was outside, and we crossed the road to the garden.'

The garden, Flora said, was like going into another world. They closed the big red front door behind them, went back down the black and white steps, crossed the tiny street and went through an iron gate set inside a tall hedge. Flora said it was like going into Narnia or something, and she could hardly even hear the city any more. There was a lawn with an old stone bench and a weeping willow tree, with a low wall at the end with another gate in it, and a pontoon on the other side, and on the pontoon there was a little table covered with food, an ice bucket with a bottle of champagne, glasses and cups and plates and a Thermos of coffee. There was jazz music playing, and one of those mini barbecues in a bucket, and cakes and croissants and pastries and the smell of cooking sausages.

'Surprise!' Zach's mother appeared suddenly from

behind the branches of the weeping willow. Zach started to laugh. Flora tried not to stare.

For today's picnic, Wanda was dressed like a society lady from the 1920s, with a cloche hat and a big fur-collared coat over a drop-waist dress, grey buttoned shoes and matching gloves. She twirled to show herself off.

'Do you like it?' she asked. 'I've got something for you too. I thought we should have fun!'

And that was how Flora found herself having the strangest picnic, sitting on a pontoon on the Thames in late January, with a feather boa round her neck and a cloche hat of her own, eating croissants and sausages and drinking champagne, with Zach sitting next to her in a straw boater and a stripy blazer.

'I didn't know if we should have breakfast or lunch,' Wanda said. 'So I made brunch!'

She made it sound like brunch was something she had just invented all on her own.

'Did she even mention Mum?' I asked, and Flora said no, but that at this point everything was so strange and rather wonderful she wasn't even thinking about Mum either. That came later, Flora said.

After they'd eaten, Wanda taught Zach and Flora

to dance the Charleston, still on the pontoon. Then when the wind started to whip up on the river, they carried everything back to the garden and sat under the willow tree, where she and Zach reminisced about all the other picnics they'd had there, and she made Flora laugh by telling stories of the scrapes Zach got into when he was little.

'You see,' Zach said, putting his arm round Flora's shoulders. 'I knew you two would get along.'

'There was a flash in her eye,' Flora said. 'An actual flash. Zach didn't see it because he is so besotted with her, but I did. And that was when I remembered Mum.'

Wanda said, speaking of Flora, 'She's charming, Zach. I'm so glad I got the chance to meet her before I go away tomorrow.' Zach said, 'What do you mean, before you go away tomorrow?' and Wanda said she had been invited to stay with some friends in northern Spain who owned a delightful hotel up in the mountains.

'But you've only just got back from France!' Zach said.

'I'm afraid it can't be helped, my darling,' Wanda replied. 'I'm sailing on tomorrow's boat. That's why I wanted to see you today.'

'Who goes to Spain by boat?' I asked.

'Loads of people, apparently,' Flora said. 'That's kind of not the point.'

'But what about me?' Zach asked when Wanda said about the boat, and Flora's blood started to boil because he looked so miserable. 'Where will I live?'

Wanda replied that Zach seemed to be very happy living where he was.

'I can't stay with Zoran for ever,' Zach said.

'Can't you stay here on your own?'

'No,' Flora snapped. 'He can't.'

'You're my family, Mum,' Zach insisted.

'Well your grandfather doesn't seem to think so,' Wanda said.

'And that's when I left,' Flora concluded. 'I couldn't stand it. She really is a witch, Blue. She puts spells on people. She almost put a spell on *me*, with her music and her clothes and her fancy picnic. His little face when she said that she was leaving again! He walked me back to the end of the street and I tried to tell him what she was doing but he wouldn't listen. I said she was playing us, him against his grandfather, him against me. I said she doesn't care about anyone but herself, she only told you about Spain because you were talking about me and she can't stand it not being all about her.'

'What did Zach say?'

'That I was wrong and that she loves him. Didn't I see how she was today? Would she really have put on a picnic like that if she didn't love him, if she didn't want to impress me? I said she'd have impressed me more if she'd bothered to apologise about hurling stones at my mother.'

'How did he react to that?'

'He said we have to look after her. I said no, *you* have to look after her. She's not my problem, and maybe Dad's right, maybe we shouldn't see each other for a while. I told him to call me when he'd got over his mother complex, and that I was going back to my own family.'

'You said that? "Call me when you're over your mother complex"?'

Flora gave a tiny smile. 'It's not quite a milkshake, but seriously, I'm tired of always hearing about her. I can't believe I ever thought it was more important to protect Zach than tell the truth to Dad. There's no one more important than you all, no one.'

Sometimes I really love my big sister, but she is always so extreme.

'I can't believe Wanda never mentioned Mum to you,' I said. 'And I'm really pleased you stood up for us and everything, but don't you think that now *you* are being unfair on Zach?'

Flora looked worried. 'Do you think so?'

'A little bit.'

'I'll call him tomorrow,' she said. 'He'll need cheering up anyway if that witch really is leaving. Also, do you think I should tell Dad what happened today? I'm tired of secrets. And Jas will be relieved to know Wanda's leaving.'

'He'll be furious with you for disobeying him, but yeah, I think you should.'

'I'll go right now, before I lose my nerve.' She opened the door. The sound of Dad and Jas yelling at each other floated up from the kitchen. Flora caught my eye and we both started to laugh.

'Maybe not right now,' I suggested.

I grabbed my camera and together we tiptoed downstairs to see what was going on.

The Film Diaries of Bluebell Gadsby

Scene Eight (Transcript)
The Headless Corpse
Or, The Inevitable Outcome of Releasing Your Pets

INTERIOR. DAY.

Screaming grows louder as CAMERAMAN (Blue) enters the Gadsby kitchen, where FATHER is holding RON and HERMIONE by the scruff of the neck. JASMINE jumps up and down around him trying to catch the kittens, who contort their bodies as they seek to escape, meowing piteously. On the floor lie the smashed remains of a fruit bowl, two kitchen chairs, several oranges, a squashed banana and a decapitated baby rat. TWIG sits on the sofa, watching in awed fascination.

                    JAS
                 (screams)
    IT'S YOUR FAULT! IT'S YOUR FAULT!!
    YOU SHOULDN'T HAVE LET THEM GO!!!

                  FATHER
               (also screams)
    YOU HAVE NO WAY OF KNOWING THESE ARE
    YOUR BABY RATS! THEY COULD BE ANY
    BABY RATS!! AND ANYWAY, IT WASN'T ME
            WHO KILLED THEM!!!

                    JAS
                 (roars)
    BETSY WAS PREGNANT WHEN YOU LET HER
    ESCAPE! WHY ELSE WOULD THERE BE BABY
            RATS IN OUR GARDEN?

                   TWIG
    Face it, Dad, you pulled the trigger
                 yourself.

              JAS and FATHER
               SHUT UP, TWIG!

                  FATHER
             (a little more calmly)

                    230

It is *not* my fault that this house
is overrun by rodents and murderous
felines.

JAS
(snarls)
This would never have happened if
they were safe in their cage!

FLORA
(entering kitchen after Blue)
OH MY GOD THERE'S A RAT WITHOUT A
HEAD!!

Flora joins the debris on the floor in
a dead faint. Father drops the kittens
and starts to slap her. The kittens
pounce on the dead baby rat and drag
it, snarling, under the dresser.

FATHER
I want those creatures gone by
tonight.

JAS
(now hysterical)
Daddy, please!

FLORA
(returns to consciousness)
Where am I?

FATHER
IF THEY'RE NOT GONE BY MORNING, I
WILL TAKE THEM TO THE PET SHOP! FIRST
MY SHOES AND NOW A HEADLESS CORPSE!!
WHAT IS WRONG WITH THIS FAMILY? CAN
NO ONE ELSE SEE HOW WRONG THIS IS???

Dad's phone rang then and he stopped yelling because it was Mum calling from upstairs, telling him to stop shouting and also asking for a cup of tea. Flora staggered across to the sofa and said she felt sick and wanted tea too. Twig passed her a bucket. Jas sat down next to her and glared at Dad until he left.

'I thought he liked the kittens now,' she said.

'I don't think he likes anyone or anything right at the moment,' Flora said.

'Will he really take them to the pet shop?'

'I think he's almost as mad as Zach's mother,' Flora replied.

Twig started doing angry Dad impersonations, scratching under his arms like a monkey and going, 'I've got fleas! Who pooed in my shoes?'

'It's not funny,' said Jas.

'I've had a brilliant idea,' I said.

They all turned towards me, looking expectant. I do love it when they do that.

'We'll take them to Gloria,' I announced.

'That's your brilliant idea?' said Twig. 'Are you sure she likes kittens?'

'They can be stable cats,' I said. 'They'd love that,

Jas. They're half wild anyway, and you can visit them every week. You know if they stay here they'll only keep on hunting down the rats. This way, the babies will get to grow up, *and* the kittens will be happy.'

Jas said my idea *was* brilliant, and that if Ron and Hermione couldn't live with us, there was nobody in the world she would rather they live with than Gloria. She wanted to take them right away.

'We'll go tomorrow,' I said. 'It's already getting dark and I'm not getting murdered in that alley, not even for Ron and Hermione.'

'Dad said they had to be gone tonight.'

'I've had an idea for that too.'

'Not again,' groaned Zoran when Jas, Twig and I turned up at his flat complete with two kittens and their litter tray and sleeping box. 'How many times do I have to say no?'

'One night,' I said.

'Dad's banished them,' Twig explained.

'Like Zach,' Jas added.

'Where is Zach, by the way?' I asked.

Zoran said he was in the shower.

'Is he OK?' I asked.

'Well he's not exactly tap-dancing and singing show tunes, but he's doing all right. Why?'

'Nothing,' I said.

If Zach hasn't told Zoran about his mum, there's no way I'm getting involved.

Back home, I told Dad our plans about the kittens. I thought maybe he would grant a last-minute reprieve, like they do in books, but he didn't. Jas has also appealed to Mum one last time, but Mum says she doesn't want to upset Dad.

Zoran is meeting us tomorrow at the Tube station.

The Film Diaries of Bluebell Gadsby

Scene Nine (Transcript)
Kitten Handover

EXTERIOR. DAY. STREET SCENE, OUTSIDE
A TUBE STATION.

ZORAN stands waiting at the entrance
to the Tube station, holding a
cardboard box, which emits loud meows
and hisses. Passers-by glance at him
curiously. Zoran wears a thick leather
jacket, leather gloves and motorcycle
boots. There is a vivid red scratch on
his left cheek.
  JASMINE takes the box from him and
coos at it. Zoran glares at it
malevolently. The box hisses louder.

ZORAN
Are you sure Gloria is going to want
these horrors?

                    TWIG
        Personally, I have my doubts.

                   JASMINE
                  (offended)
            They are not horrors.

             CAMERAMAN (BLUE)
           (with fake breeziness)
        Everybody loves kittens. Are you
                coming with us?

                    ZORAN
          I feel I should. I'd feel
    responsible if anything happened to
    you on the Tube with those charming
              creatures in tow.

Cut to the entrance of the stable
yard. Zoran, Twig, Jas, Cameraman and
cardboard box are gathered outside the
gate. The sky is bright blue and their
breath comes out in little frozen
puffs. Even the alleyway looks almost
pretty in the sunshine. A clump of

snowdrops has come out in the tiny
patch of earth under the chestnut tree.

CAMERAMAN
(still being positive)
Nothing bad can happen on a day like
today.

As one body, they turn into the yard,
where ponies hang their heads over the
doors of their boxes. BILL sits checking
the straps on riding hats. GLORIA
strides about looking splendid in
skin-tight jodhpurs, drinking coffee
and carrying a pitchfork.
Zoran gazes at her.

GLORIA
(kindly, to Jas, not appearing to
notice Zoran)
You're a little early for your
lesson, aren't you? What's in the box?

JAS
(suddenly unsure, casting imploring
glances at Cameraman)
They're, um . . . well . . . sort of . . .

Box meows loudly.

                    ZORAN
              (still gazing)
     We were wondering if you might . . .

                  CAMERAMAN
     We thought in case you had mice . . .

                    TWIG
     They're very good at killing rats.

                  JASMINE
     (glares at Twig, before squaring her
     shoulders to announce confidently)
          They are my kittens, and I would
     like them to come and live with you.

Gloria's mouth twitches. Zoran places
the cardboard box on the floor. Gloria
and Bill approach. Jas lifts up the
lid. Two black kitten heads pop up,
ears pricked, green eyes flashing like
lightning, oversized whiskers twitching
indignantly. HERMIONE is the first out.
She leaps cleanly over the top of the
box and pads cautiously into the yard,

sniffing. RON, who is fatter and clumsier, clips the edge of the box, falls to the ground, turns a somersault and follows his sister with his short tail held high, like he missed his entrance on purpose.

Camera swings to Gloria. The expression on her face confirms fears that she is not a kitteny person. She stares at them, baffled.

GLORIA
You're bringing me kittens?

ZORAN
(trying to be ingratiating)
We thought they might be useful.

GLORIA
But what am I going to do with . . .

She is interrupted by a new noise, a sort of wheezing, rumbling, spluttering sound, so unexpected it takes a moment to locate where it is coming from.

It is the sound of Bill, laughing.

Bill crouches down. Hermione, sensing a friend, marches up to him and rubs her face against his leg. Ron, not to be outdone, follows. Bill unmistakably coos.

Unlike his daughter, it appears he *is* a kitteny person.

GLORIA
(face softening at the sight of her father petting kittens)
Have they had all their vaccinations yet?

Her eyes meet Zoran's for the first time and she blushes.

I'm writing this from the back of the car.

It was sweet, watching Zoran and Gloria connect like that, their eyes locking over a box full of kittens. I kind of wish Dodi had been there. It would have thrilled her romantic heart, but given everything that happened afterwards, it feels like it took place almost in another life.

Gloria's blush only lasted about three seconds, but we all saw it.

'We met at Jas's poetry competition,' Zoran stammered.

Twig sniggered. I kicked him. Mopsy tried to sniff Hermione, who scratched him on the nose, Ron found a corner to wee in, Jas and Bill wandered off into the tack room to find a place for the kittens' bed. And Flora turned up on Zoran's scooter.

'What the ****?' I thought Zoran's eyes were going to pop out of his head, and who can blame him, when one moment he is gazing goofily at Gloria and the next his hot-headed ex-charge who for all he knows has never ridden a scooter in her life turns up driving his personal property.

'Never mind all that!' Flora cried. 'Zach has disappeared!'

'What do you mean?' cried Zoran.

'He's not answering his phone.'

'But that doesn't mean . . .'

'Will you just listen to me!' Flora shouted. Then she clambered off the scooter, took a deep breath, and told us what had happened.

'I argued with Zach yesterday,' she said. 'But this morning, when I woke up, I wanted to say I was sorry. So I rang him.'

Flora being Flora, it wasn't enough for her just to leave a message. Instead, knowing he was working at the record shop this morning, she decided to pay him a surprise visit.

'But your father,' Zoran said. 'You're not supposed to see . . .'

'Please,' said Flora.

Even though it was still early, the shop owner was already there, but he told her Zach had called in sick. So then she decided to call on Zach to minister to him on his sick bed, but when she got to Zoran's there was nobody there. She found the emergency key Zoran keeps hidden in a loose brick in the wall for whenever Zach forgets his ('That's supposed to be a secret!' Zoran said, but she ignored him) and let herself into the flat, which was when she saw that Zach's things were gone, his clothes and his guitar and everything. So she panicked, grabbed Zoran's helmet and the keys to his scooter and rode over to Zach's grandfather's house.

'Why?' Zoran asked.

'In case his mum was there,' I explained. 'Flora spent the day with them yesterday.'

'What! Why does nobody tell me anything?' Zoran sounded exasperated and furious and disappointed all at once.

'He sounds just like Dad,' Twig whispered.

'I wanted to last night, but I thought it would be better if Zach did,' I explained.

'You saw Zach's mum yesterday?' Jas asked Flora. She looked at me. *And you knew?*'

'Is anyone listening to a word I'm saying?' Flora shouted.

'Carry on,' ordered Zoran.

'There was nobody at the house. I rang the doorbell, and I checked in the garden, and then I shouted up at the window to Zach's room, and eventually a neighbour came out and said, if I was looking for Zach I was too late, because he had gone. He saw him leave this morning with Wanda and a rucksack and a guitar.'

Zoran was looking really confused.

'But he was asleep at home when I left!'

'Did you check on him?' I asked.

'I just assumed,' he admitted. Poor Zoran was shaking. Gloria took command.

'Where do you think he has gone?' she demanded.

'SPAIN!' Flora howled. 'By boat! Today!'

Twig nodded and said, 'The Portsmouth–Santander service.'

'How do you *know* that?' Gloria asked.

'I have spent a lot of time recently studying transportation,' Twig replied.

Zoran looked like he did when he lost Twig on the Tube last year, only much, much worse. Gloria said, 'We have to find out from which station and when trains leave for Portsmouth.'

'Trains to Portsmouth Harbour leave from Waterloo,' Twig said. 'There are trains all the time. The next one leaves at ten, and gets in at eleven thirty-three. Of course, they might have caught the bus, which is cheaper, but slower. I don't know the bus timetables. The ferries leave at different times every day, depending on the tides. If someone gives me a smartphone, I can look up today's sailing time.'

'Thank goodness for Maisie's little brother,' Zoran muttered as he copied down train times. His phone rang. 'Maybe it's Zach,' Zoran said hopefully, then he looked at the number. 'Oh ****, it's his grandfather.'

He walked away from us to take the call.

Gloria raised an eyebrow at me. 'Zach is the boy from the poetry competition?'

'Yes.'

'And his grandfather?'

'Is in hospital. Zoran is supposed to be looking after Zach.'

'And the reason it's a bad thing Zach is with his mother?'

'She's a witch,' said Flora. 'She keeps running away, and she tried to kill Mum.'

'I see,' Gloria said. 'And are Zach and Zoran related?'

'Not even a little bit,' I said. 'Zoran's just a very, very nice person.'

Gloria smiled.

Zoran came back from talking to Mr Rudowski, looking shaken but also quite determined. 'He wanted to know if we'd found his daughter.'

'What did he say when you said you'd lost his grandson?' asked Twig.

'He was understandably very upset,' Zoran said. 'This time he said we should call the police.'

'And tell them what?' Gloria asked. 'That a boy has run away with his mother?'

'It's all my fault!' cried Flora. 'I was mean to him! Zoran, you have to do something! He can't run away with her, she's evil!'

'I don't think she's evil,' Zoran said slowly. 'But I agree he can't go with her.'

He was holding his phone to his ear again. 'Straight to answerphone.' He started tapping out a text.

'How can you text at a time like this!'

I've never seen Flora so hysterical.

'It's important. He might read a text, even if he's not answering his phone.'

'We have to *do* something, Zoran!' Flora begged.

'Yes but what?' Zoran said.

'Find him, of course,' said Bill. Everyone turned round and looked at him like he was mad, or a genius, or maybe both.

'How?' asked Jas.

Unlike Dad, Bill copes beautifully in a crisis. 'The train station, the coach station and the harbour,' he said. 'Chances are he's left town already, but you never know. Gloria'll take Waterloo, I'll go to Victoria, you get yourself down to Portsmouth.'

'By train?' Zoran looked confused.

'Don't be daft, man! By bike!'

We all looked a little bit sceptically across to where Zoran's electric scooter was parked under the chestnut tree.

'Not that thing!' Bill grunted. He shuffled across the yard to the box right at the end of the row and threw the doors open. Inside stood what I have since discovered is a gleaming vintage Harley-Davidson.

'Mine, from a long time ago,' Bill said. 'Still goes like the wind, though you'll have to top up the fuel. You'd better get going.'

'But you? How will you get to Waterloo? To Victoria? By Tube?'

Bill laughed then, a real laugh, not a wheeze.

'How do you think we'll get there?' he roared. 'On horseback!'

And suddenly they were all running around like headless chickens.

'I'm coming with you!' Flora yelled as Zoran pulled his helmet on.

'I cannot take responsibility . . .'

'Bill, have you got a spare helmet? Leathers? Can I have some riding boots?'

'You go to Victoria, Gloria, I'll take Waterloo!'

'Flora, I said . . . oh, for God's sake, just get on!'

'I called my friend Penny who helps me

sometimes,' Gloria cried, dashing past with a bridle and saddle. 'She'll be here in about twenty minutes. Until then I'm leaving you kids in charge.'

Zoran gazed at her in admiration.

'Move!' Flora screeched.

They were all gone in less than ten minutes, in a cloud of diesel fumes and a clatter of hooves. I'm not sure it's good for horses to gallop down streets. I'm pretty certain it's illegal. But I do know I've never seen Bill look so happy.

'Do you think he really used to be a jockey?' Jas sat on the floor, cuddling Ron and Hermione, while Flopsy nibbled her sweatshirt.

'Looks like it,' I said.

'Who do you think will find him?' asked Twig.

We started trying to guess – Gloria, because she's so cool! Bill, because he's the fastest! – but our conversation was cut short when our car shrieked into the yard and Dad threw open the door, demanding to know why he had just seen Flora riding off down the street on the back of a motorbike.

I had to stop writing because I was feeling sick. I have never been so fast in a car, ever.

It only took Dad about five minutes to get the whole story out of us. The minute he heard what Flora and Zoran were doing, he yelled that he was going after them. Then he realised he had no idea how to get to Portsmouth Harbour, and needed Twig to go with him because Twig is the only one who understands how to use the SatNav. I said I wanted to go too, which meant Jas also had to come because she's too small to be left alone.

'But we have to wait for Penny,' Jas said, partly because she is a very responsible stable hand but also because she was buying time for Zoran and Flora to get away.

Once we were finally off, Dad drove like a lunatic, yelling out random sentences like 'I only came to find you because I felt bad about the kittens!' and 'Spain! Portsmouth! Motorbikes! Jesus!' and 'WhyOWhyOWhy are we having another baby?'

'I still don't understand why we are going after them,' Twig said as we roared on to the motorway.

'They might have an accident!' Dad shouted.

'Zach's mother is a maniac! Flora might run away to Spain! ANYTHING MIGHT HAPPEN!'

Dad swerved to avoid a lorry. Twig screamed.

'I am just doing what any parent would do!' Dad yelled.

'Is Daddy being a hero?' Jas whispered to me.

'In a way,' I whispered back.

We caught up with Zoran and Flora as they pulled out of a petrol station on the motorway.

'I thought motorbikes were really fast,' Jas remarked. 'How come they're not further ahead?'

'Zoran is a very responsible driver,' I said. Dad gave a short laugh, swerved again and swore.

'You can't slow down,' Twig told him. 'The ferry sails in less than an hour.'

We kept them in our sights right up until the turn-off for Portsmouth, but we lost them in the queue to the harbour, mainly because Zoran managed to avoid the traffic by riding his motorbike down the oncoming lane, which was empty. Then, when we arrived at the entrance to the harbour, Dad had to explain that we were looking for the ferry to Spain, but that we didn't have any tickets, nor did we want to buy any.

'I am looking for my daughter!' Dad cried. 'She has run away on a motorbike to find her boyfriend.'

The ticket man, whose badge said he was called Percy Williams, said that was the most exciting thing he'd heard all day, but that boarding for the *Queen Sofia* had already closed.

'We're too late!' Jas wailed.

'Let us through!' Dad snarled at Percy. 'My daughter is somewhere in this precinct and I mean to bring her home!'

Percy said he sympathised because he also had daughters, but in his experience there was not a blind bit of use trying to stop them falling in love with unsuitable boyfriends.

'You've just got to let it run its course,' Percy advised. Behind us, a long line of cars were honking their horns. 'I'm going to have to ask you to leave now.'

Dad reversed out of the line, parked the car on the side of the road and tore back past Percy's hut at a sprint, with the rest of us right behind him. Quite a few people were watching by now and a group of kids on a school trip even started to cheer.

'There's no more boats for Spain until tomorrow!' Percy shouted after us, but Dad didn't listen. He ran, and we ran after him, all the way to the waterfront, and then he stopped so suddenly we all bumped into him, because there sitting on a bollard on the quayside, looking out to sea with his rucksack at his feet and his guitar still on his back, watching the *Queen Sofia* pull out of Portsmouth Harbour, was Zach. And there also, walking towards him, clad in leather and carrying their helmets and looking like something out of a Hollywood movie, were Zoran and Flora.

Zach looked up when he heard footsteps behind him. Zoran and Flora both reached out to touch him. Zach said something we couldn't hear. Flora flung her arms around him. Zoran put his arms around them both.

Dad sniffed, loudly.

Jas announced, 'Daddy, I don't care what you say about us not being allowed to talk to Zach,' and marched over towards the hugging, huddled heap that was Zach and Zoran and Flora. Twig and I followed.

'You missed the boat,' Jas said.

'No, I didn't,' Zach whispered.

Like Grandma says, there's always a choice. Zach's choice was whether to leave or stay. And when he switched his phone back on and read Zoran's text, he made his decision.

Zoran's text said: *Ask Wanda to tell you the truth about why she left you.*

So he did. And I don't know what he said to her, but for once Wanda did tell him the truth.

After Zach's gran died, Mr Rudowski gave Wanda a choice: stay at home with them and get medical help, or leave. He said if she stayed he would help her, but that things couldn't go on as they had before, that it wasn't fair on Zach.

'The doctors would have put me on drugs,' Wanda told Zach. 'I didn't want that.'

Mr Rudowski didn't kick her out. Wanda chose to leave.

'Witch,' Flora said fiercely.

'She's not a witch,' Zach said softly. 'She's frightened.'

Flora snorted. Zoran frowned at her and she stopped.

'But why did you run away?' Jas wanted to know.

'She asked me to go with her,' Zach said.

Suddenly I remembered how lost he looked at Zoran's concert, when he realised Wanda hadn't come after all. I pictured him as a little boy, laughing with his mum at one of her crazy picnics. And then I thought of him and Mr Rudowski, living alone in the old house by the river, both missing people who weren't there, and I understood.

I guess a part of Zach will always want to be with his mum.

So Zach left. He went home to Zoran's flat, said nothing, waited till Zoran was sleeping, and crept back to his grandfather's house in the early morning.

'I was going to do it,' he said. 'All the way down on the train Mum kept talking about the mountains, about fig and apricot and almond trees, goats and beaches and blue sky. I knew even then that it was crazy, but she made it sound wonderful. Then we arrived, and I switched on my phone, and there was Zoran's text. After Mum told me the truth, all I could think about was Grandpa. He lied for her. He let me believe he'd kicked her out so I didn't know she'd chosen to leave me. And he's old and sick, he's completely lost without Grandma, and I've been so angry with him. So I said I wasn't going with her. And Mum – Mum decided to leave.'

Zach's voice wobbled, but he didn't cry. Flora hugged him even closer.

'I'm sorry,' she said.

'Me too,' he replied. 'But as someone very wise once explained to me – it's the people who stay who really matter.'

He looked at me when he said that and I felt all happy inside.

Far out at sea, the *Queen Sofia* had almost disappeared. We were all watching it: Twig, Jas and me with our feet dangling over the water, Zach on one bollard with his arms around Flora, Zoran on another. It was a big moment.

'The ones who stay, and the ones who come after you.'

Dad had crept up on us without any of us hearing.

'I'm glad you stayed, son,' he said.

Slowly, slowly, Zach smiled his amazing smile.

'Come on,' Zoran said. 'I'll buy you all something to eat.'

We turned our backs on the sea and walked across the empty quayside to the entrance to the departure area.

'No way is that yours!' Zach said, when we stopped at Bill's Harley.

'It's a long story,' Zoran said.

Twig's phone rang while we were arguing about who should ride into town with Zoran. 'It's for you,' he said, handing it to me. 'It's that mad cow you call your best friend.'

'Tell Twig I heard that,' Dodi said. 'And where *are* you?'

'Portsmouth,' I grinned.

'What? Where even *is* that? Listen, Jake's had an idea.'

I let Dodi talk. Flora and Zach were sitting together on the motorbike. Dad was on his phone to Mum, trying to explain what had happened, and Jas was on Zoran's phone talking to Gloria. Flora wrapped her arms around Zach and whispered something in his ear. They both laughed. The sun was shining. The sea was blue. It was perfect.

'Tomorrow then,' Dodi was saying.

'Sure,' I smiled, and hung up.

Zoran rode into town with Zach, and we all followed behind.

The Film Diaries of Bluebell Gadsby

Scene Ten (Transcript)
Criminal Activity

EXTERIOR. PRE-DAWN. THE PLAYGROUND OF
CLARENDON FREE SCHOOL.

JAKE, COLIN, TOM, DODI and CAMERAMAN (Blue)
have just scaled the school gates and huddle
beneath the window of the staff common room.

> CAMERAMAN (BLUE)
> Won't it be locked?

> JAKE
> (proud of himself)
> Shouldn't be. I slipped in during Saturday
> detention and stole the window bolts.

> CAMERAMAN
> But isn't there an alarm?

                         DODI
        Blue, stop being so *negative*! Jake's
          thought of everything! He's got
        thirty seconds before it goes off.

                      CAMERAMAN
                   Thirty seconds!

                         JAKE
        (assuming the air of a Commando officer
        and brandishing a pair of wire cutters)
          All right, lads. I'm going in.

Colin   gives   him   a   leg-up   to   the
windowsill. Jake crouches on the ledge. It
looks for a moment as if he will lose his
balance and fall, but then he grins down at
his friends on the ground and they realise
that he is showing off. He pushes the sash
open and reaches down for the camera.

                   CAMERAMAN (JAKE)
        And so our intrepid explorer ventures
        into the scary depths of the staff common
        room. This is the den where Maths teachers

lurk, the natural habitat of child-eating French teachers . . . And here, if our bold adventurer is not mistaken, is said French teacher's locker.

Picture is reduced to blurred image of common-room floor as Jake fumbles in his rucksack. Off camera, there is the sound of heavy breathing, and a sharp click as metal cutters cut through a padlock.

> CAMERAMAN (JAKE)
> Eureka!

A pair of gloved hands picks through the contents of the locker – books, notebooks, a printed scarf, perfume, two bottles of Evian, a packet of crackers and a cardboard box containing lipsticks, tissues and an assortment of confiscated telephones. Jake grabs the lot and stuffs them into his rucksack. The screech of a burglar alarm splits the air. Picture goes mad as Jake vaults out of the window.

> CAMERAMAN (JAKE)
> RUN!

I've never run so fast or laughed so much while I was running. We raced to the school gate, scrambled over it and kept on running until we reached the park, where we collapsed on a bench, panting and still laughing. Jake reached into his rucksack and pulled out Mme Gilbert's box of lipsticks and phones.

'One of these is yours, I believe, milady,' he said.

'I can't believe you just did that!' I said, taking the box.

'Anything for you, Blue,' Jake said, and that is when I noticed the way that Dodi was looking at him, like he was some kind of superhero.

Dodi likes Jake. I can't believe I never realised before.

Mum came downstairs today. Now that Dad has developed a taste for being heroic, he wanted to carry her down from her bedroom, but she wouldn't let him. Instead he has been driving her mad with his fussing, but you can see that she actually loves it. And Zoran came round on his way back from the stables. His excuse for going over was to pick up his scooter and also to pay the fines Gloria and Bill got for galloping their horses across London looking for Zach, but when he came back he couldn't stop grinning.

Gloria is going to give him riding lessons.

As for Zach, he has finished writing his song for Flora. He played it to her this afternoon in the tree house, and when they came down her eyes were shining. Zach says he's going to play it at Zoran's next concert, but I'm not allowed to film it. And my point about all this is these people, one way or another, are all in love. And however many phones Jake steals for me or how many roses he gives me, nothing is going to change the fact that I just don't feel that way about him. So this afternoon I went round to Jake's house and did something I should have done a long time ago.

'If it's because of Tallulah,' Jake said, 'I promise that is completely over.'

'It's not about Tallulah,' I said. Then, because I had promised myself I was going to be truthful, I added, 'I mean it's not *completely* about Tallulah. I just don't want to go out with you. I never *did* want to go out with you in the first place. I only said yes because it felt a bit awkward to say no, which if you think about it is a completely rubbish basis for a relationship. You're amazing because you're the sort of brilliant person who is prepared to break into school to steal back a phone, but please can we just be friends again?'

It all came out in a rush and I did feel a bit bad because of the criminal activity and everything, but I think he finally got the message. Afterwards I went round to Dodi's house to tell her. I could see she was secretly pleased, but she said, 'You're mad, everyone wants a boyfriend.'

'Well I am not everyone,' I said.

'I bet this time next week you'll be back together with him.'

I didn't have a milkshake handy, but there was a bottle of water on the table. 'You wouldn't dare,' Dodi said, but I did. I chased her all round her garden with it and only stopped when she was so wet you could see her bra through her T-shirt.

Boys can wait. Friends are way more fun.

Saturday 8 March

People only write in diaries when things are going badly. And lately things have been good.

I had a long chat with Dodi after I'd spoken to Jake, and she admitted that she has liked him for ages, ever since she spent so much time talking to him about me. She said she would never go out with him if I minded even the tiniest bit. I told her that I would mind a *lot* if she didn't. They have been together for nearly a month now, and they really are the cutest couple. Now that Jake has found a girl who adores him and who doesn't live in a different hemisphere, he has become the model boyfriend.

Zoran and Gloria – well, let's just say their relationship has extended beyond riding lessons . . .

Ron and Hermione kill every rodent that crosses their paths at the stables. Which is nice for them, if not for the rodents.

Jas and Bill have become best friends and are writing poetry together.

Twig finally understood Maisie Carter was just using him as a free babysitting service, and is now pining for a new girl called Bianca.

Flora and Zach are more in love than ever, and Mr Rudowski has come home.

Me? There's nothing new. And that's just fine. Life's good. Boring. No surprises.

EXCEPT TODAY!!!!

TODAY WAS VERY, VERY, VERY EXCITING.

Today, for the first time, we met Mr Rudowski.

The Film Diaries of Bluebell Gadsby

Scene Eleven (Transcript)
Mr Rudowski Comes for Dinner

INTERIOR. EVENING.

On the top floor of 32 Chatsworth Square, FLORA paces her bedroom, trying on and throwing down clothes, wailing things like *What shall I wear? I have no clothes! Oh what am I supposed to wear?* Pan to kitchen, where MOTHER moves heavily about. For once, the kitchen is not a mess. A stew bubbles gently on the stove. A salad nestles in a bowl on the table, which is perfectly laid with mostly unchipped china. A pan of boiled potatoes sits on the side, waiting to be mashed. Mother grunts as she bends down to check on the pineapple cake in the oven.

MOTHER
(murmuring)
Perfect.

Mother waddles over to the sofa and falls asleep.

Pan to study, where FATHER sits hunched over his laptop, typing with a look of furious concentration.

Pan to landing, where TWIG sits on the floor, practising card tricks on JAS.

JAS
Do you really think card tricks are going to impress her?

TWIG
Everybody loves card tricks.

Front door bell rings. Flora appears on the landing, wearing a navy blue trouser suit, sensible shoes, a silk scarf around her neck and a slash of fuchsia lipstick.

                    FLORA
                 How do I look?

                     JAS
                 (awestruck)
            Really, really *boring*.

                    TWIG
            Except for the lipstick. The
            lipstick makes you look mad.

Downstairs, Mother (now awake) has opened
the door to ZORAN, GLORIA, ZACH and MR
RUDOWSKI. Mr Rudowski wears a trilby, a
natty blazer and a spotted bow tie. Gloria
is magnificent in her usual skin-tight
black and glossy knee-high boots.

                MR RUDOWSKI
        (raising Mother's hand to his lips)
        Mrs Gadsby, thank you for inviting
         me to dinner. I have heard so much
                about you from Zach.

                    ZACH
         (looking up, spotting Flora on the
                   landing)

                     267

Flora, come and meet Grandpa!

FLORA
(wailing)
I can't, I have to get changed!

FATHER
(bursting out of his study)
I finished my book! I finished my
book!

The fire alarm goes off. Black smoke
begins to waft up from the kitchen.

MOTHER
I forgot the cake!

ZORAN
(to Mr Rudowski)
I'm afraid they're often like this.

Mother starts to waddle towards the
kitchen but suddenly stops with a
startled squeak. All turn to look at
her. She stands in a state of shock,
looking down at her bump.

                    MOTHER
        I think my waters have broken!

                    FATHER
        Call the midwife! Put the kettle on!
            Where are my car keys?

He runs upstairs, shouting something
about Mother's hospital bag. Mother
watches him go and smiles. Then, as her
first contraction starts, she winces.
The contraction passes. She smiles
again.

                    MOTHER
        Turn the camera off, Blue.

Q&A

Get to know Natasha Farrant...

How long did it take you to write *Flora in Love*?

The first draft took me about a year. Then another six months of rewrites and edits.

Did you grow up in a big family? If so, what was it like?

I have two sisters, a brother, twelve first cousins and lots of second cousins, aunts, uncles and people who for years I thought were family members but turned out just to be friends. On the one hand, being part of a big family is wonderful. I love the chaos and surprise of never knowing quite who is going to come through the door next, and the sense of belonging to a large, noisy clan. On the other hand, though, it does mean you have to shout quite loud to be heard, and sometimes that can be difficult.

Why did you decide to add a new baby to the Gadsby family?

I was eighteen years old when my brother was born, four years after my second sister. I think it's fascinating what babies do to families: they can bring everyone together, but they also turn everything upside down and make everyone question their own feelings and how they fit in. I look at this more closely in the next Bluebell book.

You grew up in London. What was it like growing up there?

I loved growing up in London. It's such a buzzy, lively, exciting place. I did most of my schooling at the French Lycée, and it was brilliant to be part of a community that spoke lots of different languages: not just French and English but also Arabic, Spanish, Italian, German . . . I loved that there were so many cinemas and parks and places where I could meet my friends, and that everything was just a tube or a bus ride away. My parents also took us to the theatre a lot, which I really enjoyed. And I was very lucky. We lived in a flat that looked over a tennis club. My parents were great tennis players, and that club with its huge garden became our playground, where we would meet lots of other neighbourhood kids and run wild until after it got dark. I don't think it's like that any more though – I think it's become a lot more chi-chi...

Where did the inspiration for Zoran's character come from?

Mary Poppins, initially. I love Poppins. And my kids briefly had a male nanny. He was French and a musician, and very nice, but he didn't stay very long – he was more interested in his music than in looking after children.

Do you remember your first kiss?

Yes. But I don't want to talk about it!

Who is your favourite Gadsby child?

Jas. I know I probably shouldn't have favourites, but she just is.

Were your parents anything like Bluebell's mum and dad?

I think the Gadsby parents are like a lot of parents,

actually. They're doing the best they can, sometimes they get it right, sometimes they get it wrong.

Did you ever have a crush on your sister's boyfriend?

I don't want to talk about that either!

Have you ever written any poetry?

Yes. It was very bad but also very sad. It was about my grandfather dying. It actually helped me quite a lot at the time, but I've never thought of writing more, even though I really love poetry. It's like painting with words. Just, I'm not a very good painter!

If you could go back in time to any film ever made, which film would you most like to see on a first date?

I don't have to go back in time much at all, actually. *Despicable Me*. I just saw it and I haven't laughed so much for ages. It's a perfect first-date film: if the person you see it with doesn't find it funny, he's not for you. Ditto if he doesn't think Agnes is adorable, or if he doesn't speak in minion language for days afterwards.

What's the best Christmas present you've ever received from a boyfriend? And the worst?

I can only remember Christmas presents from my husband. The worst present was an orange squeezer. It was just so disappointing. The best is still in the future. I would really, really like him to give me a Dachshund puppy (I know puppies are not really Christmas presents, but I would take super good care of it). Maybe now that I have put this down *in writing* he will do it . . .

Why did you decide that Zach would end up not following his mother?

Sadly, though family can be a wonderful, wonderful thing, that isn't always the case. Zach's longing for his mother is the most normal thing in the world, but he has the courage to realise that she will never be the person he wants her to be. She's perfectly happy for him to leave everything behind to follow her, but she would never do the same for him. It's all on her terms, and if Zach is to grow as a person –

which he has to do, to live a happy life – he has to let her go.

What's your definition of family?

People who are there for you no matter what and who love you unconditionally.

What's the best thing about being a writer? And the worst?

The best bit is getting to make up worlds in my head. The worst bit is worrying other people won't like them.

Who are your favourite children's authors at the moment?

Hilary McKay. Katherine Rundell. A little bit older, for YA, Rainbow Rowell.

When do you know you've had a good idea for a book?

When I can't sleep because I'm so excited about it. Sometimes I can lie plotting for hours in the middle of the night.

You have two teenage daughters. Do you ask them for advice?

Yes! I'm working on a new *Bluebell Gadsby*, and they are giving me chapter-by-chapter commentary. They and their friend are also helping me develop a completely new idea.

If you could have written any book besides the ones you already have, which one would it have been?

Ballet Shoes.

Why is writing important to you?

As another writer once said, 'The only thing worse than writing is not writing.' Writing is lonely, frustrating and very, very hard work but it's how I make sense of the world and even though I grumble about it, I love it. Not writing would be much easier, but it would make me miserable.

What's the best advice you've ever been given – as an author, and in life?

'Don't look at your hill. Climb it.' This was written

on a slip of paper and hung by the door of my grandmother's house in Wales, and even as a grown-up I always used to stop and read it. Basically it means stop thinking about things but get out there and make them happen instead. It is very good advice for everyone, but especially for writers because we could spend the whole day looking out of the window and daydreaming.

Are you able to tell us anything about the next book in the *Bluebell Gadsby* series?

Yes! It will be set in Dartmoor, at Grandma's house, during the summer holidays, and it opens just after Jas has dropped the new baby on its head. There are more horses (wild), two new boys (interesting) and possibly a wedding (not telling whose).